Healer Man

Don Manor is injured and grieving when he meets Callum McGeachin, the small Scotsman with an impish grin and a warm heart. Callum helps him to recover, and Don grows close to his new friend, even though there is something uncanny about him. Callum has a gift for healing, and a power that others can sense.

The two drift a while through Colorado, until they meet a widow with a sick child, a run-down ranch, and neighbours who want her land. They decide to help: Don because he hates bullies, and Callum because he's fallen in love at first sight. Rustlers are the first problem, but trouble with the neighbouring Kershaws begins to increase. Don must grow and find something new in himself to help Callum defend his love, no matter what the cost to themselves.

Healer Man

Gillian F. Taylor

A Black Horse Western

ROBERT HALE

© Gillian F. Taylor 2019
First published in Great Britain 2019

ISBN 978-0-7198-3047-1

The Crowood Press
The Stable Block
Crowood Lane
Ramsbury
Marlborough
Wiltshire SN8 2HR

www.bhwesterns.com

Robert Hale is an imprint
of The Crowood Press

The right of Gillian F. Taylor to be identified as
author of this work has been asserted by her
in accordance with the Copyright, Designs and
Patents Act 1988

Typeset by
Derek Doyle & Associates, Shaw Heath
Printed and bound in Great Britain by
4Bind Ltd, Stevenage, SG1 2XT

Dedicated to the Faith Healer, Alex Harvey.

CHAPTER ONE

I can remember clear as anything, how it all started, back at the tail end of winter, so many years ago. Me and my brother, Abe, we were working for the Bar S. It was a good little family-owned beef outfit up on the Uncompahgre Plateau, in western Colorado. We'd been part of the Bar S for a couple of years, and back then I thought I'd be there a few years more.

That late winter day, Abe and I were out together, hunting up lost cows from all the little valleys and draws. In summer, the valley pastures got rested, and Bibs Selby, who owned the Bar S, had started putting fields to hay and planting alfalfa, to feed the stock through winter. Every fall though, we brought the beef down from the higher ranges so they had some shelter to see them through the winter. Of course the cows scattered, and us hands had to keep riding out to chase them back closer to the ranch. In a month or two they would be calving, and there was still the risk of a late snowfall which could freeze a new calf in no time. Beef cows are the stubbornest, stupidest critters I know. In summer they get trapped in bogs, in winter they drift with snow and freeze to death piled against fences. They get their noses stuck full of porcupine quills and try to horn you when you pull the quills out.

So Abe and I were out like usual, looking out for the cows. It was a fine, crisp day, when we rode out together for the last time. Abe took deep breaths of that clear air as we rode in the sunshine. He smiled at me, and laughed, and we let our horses race across a grassy meadow that stretched for a way beside the river.

'That sure worked the bedsprings out some!' he whooped as we drew up. My buckskin, Luke, snorted and pulled gently on the reins. I held him down to a jog and turned his head to a side valley.

'Best save some of that sass for chasing cows,' I said, smiling.

'Iffen we ever find any of the fool critters,' Abe responded. He nudged his grey ahead of my horse and I let him take the lead, as usual.

Abe was near on two years younger than me, Don, and he'd growed up into a fine young man. Folks could always tell we were brothers. Our pappy was white, and our mamma was half darkie,

8

and half Cherokee Indian. Abe and me both had the same high cheekbones, narrow noses, and dark eyes that kind of slanted slightly. We both had straight black hair and brown skin. I used to look out for Abe when other kids picked on us for being mixed, and I never could stand for any kind of bullying.

We rode on up the little valley, watching and listening as we went. A pine squirrel chattered angrily at us, then rushed up a young tree, its tail rippling behind it. The valley curved here and there, filled with stands of aspen, pine and mountain ash. With the dense trees, and the undergrowth of juniper, alder, chokecherry and bearberry, there were plenty of places for our cows to hide in. But we couldn't find any.

I emerged from a clump of undergrowth into an open, grassy patch, and stopped to let Abe catch up. Luke dropped his head to snatch mouthfuls of grass while I rubbed my thigh where a branch had poked me as we pushed our way through. Abe came out from between two close-growing lodgepole pines, bent low along his horse's neck as the branches tugged at him. I could hear him cursing, and I was about to call out to him, when I heard something else. It was a cow bellowing, not so far up the valley. Abe heard it too; he sat upright and grinned at me. Another cow answered the first, and I thought I heard yet another.

9

'There's our beef,' Abe said happily as he rode up.

'Sounds like something's disturbing them,' I answered, my mind full of possibilities.

'Let's go see,' Abe answered simply. He nudged his grey into a jog. I pulled up Luke's head and followed.

The valley curved to the right, around an outcrop of reddish rock with pines growing from cracks in the almost sheer wall. We rode around at a steady jog, our horses' hoofs muffled by the soft footing. I remember the scent of bruised pine needles in my nostrils as we passed through a stand of trees that temporarily blocked our view ahead. Abe was sitting comfortably in that saddle with the carved fancywork on the skirts he was so proud of. He held the reins lightly in one hand, the grey going sweetly for him. Both of them full of life, and strong, there in the dappled, pale sunlight. Then we reached the edge of the trees and Abe pulled up sharp.

The sound of the cows had been getting louder, and as I drew up level with Abe, one of them let out a sharp, pain-filled bellow. The breeze brought me the smell of scorched hair and hide, and I knew what was happening even before my eyes could take it in. Four men had rounded up a dozen or so cows and were branding them. Or rather, rebranding them. I recognized the black

10

and white steer with a broken horn, even before I saw the Bar S on its hip. A red cow was scrambling to her feet, her brand altered to read Circle HS and her left ear bleeding where it had been cut with a new mark. Abe and I had stumbled on to a nest of rustlers, right in the act of stealing our outfit's cows.

Shamed as I am to say it, I didn't know what to do. I remember the shock, when I understood what we'd seen. I remember those men turning to look at us, and one of them shouting something. There was only two of us against four of them, and I wondered whether to turn and ride back to the ranch for help. But the cow thieves would be long gone afore we could get back. While I dithered, Abe acted. He yanked his old Colt from its holster high against his hip, and spurred his grey forward, yelling like a mad thing. The rustlers were already moving, scattering. Abe let off a couple of rounds at the nearest one. I never knew where they hit; it wasn't the rustler, anyhow. A mounted rustler was pulling out his rifle and slinging it to his shoulder. I heard more gunfire crack and the cows started to panic. They bellowed and started to mill around, hooking their horns at anything in reach.

As Abe raced across the open ground to the rustlers' fire, I suddenly knew I had to go along of him. Luke was tossing his head, and when I clamped my heels into his sides, he bounded forwards. Abe was firing some more, but neither of us was the sort who liked to spend money on lead to fire at targets. We carried our guns to kill snakes, and finish off injured cows and horses. Maybe iffen I had rode out there at the same time, firing my gun too, we could have scared those rustlers off, and maybe winged one of them. By the time I acted, it was too late. There was the sharp bark of a rifle, and Abe's head jerked. I still think I saw the blood spray out as the bullet crashed through his skull. The reins fell from his hand and he slid sidewards. His feet were tangled in the stirrups as his head and shoulders hit the ground, limp as a rag doll. The grey horse went on galloping, heading straight towards the man that had killed Abe. My brother's body bounced over the rough ground as it dragged alongside of his horse.

I think I screamed something but what I next remember clearly is a heavy blow, low on the left side of my belly. I don't know if I turned Luke around, or if he turned of himself. We were galloping back through the stands of trees and over patches of open ground. I was clinging to the saddle horn, and it was starting to get difficult to breathe. My belly and side ached so badly, and my shirt seemed clammy and damp. I let my horse run as he would. Branches snatched at me, tearing my clothes and stealing my hat. I don't know how long it was before I got so dizzy I could hardly stay in the saddle. Luke had slowed down by then. I remember the effort of raising my head to look around, and seeing that we were no longer in the little side valley. Sometime around then, I passed out.

I don't know how long it was till I opened my eyes again. When I think back, I remember how shafts of light came in through the trees, and gilded where they touched, so it must have been late afternoon. I was lying stretched out on a bedroll, with a blanket tucked around my legs and my coat over that. The camp was in a small clearing between crowds of aspens, and I could see my horse, unsaddled, grazing beside a bay mustang. I tried to move and pain surged up from my belly, making me cry out. At that same moment, a hand touched my shoulder gently, and a voice with an unfamiliar accent said:

'Lay quiet there now, laddie.'

I carefully turned my head just enough to see Callum for the first time. He was kneeling by my side, his shaggy black hair framing his rough face and almost hiding the dark eyes that studied me intently. Pain-racked and disorientated as I was, I still felt the power in those deep-set eyes. I took a long, slow breath and watched as he cut open my blood-soaked shirt and the flannels underneath. Too weak to move, I let a stranger carefully peel back the warm, damp layers to expose the bullet

13

wound. He studied the torn flesh, and the flows of half-congealed blood for a few moments, then turned to me. Once again I felt the power of his eyes looking into mine as he spoke.

'D'ye trust me, laddie?'

His accent was strange, guttural, and yet musical all at once. I blinked at him, not knowing what to think.

'D'ye trrust me?' He spoke more urgently, rolling his 'rrr's' as he emphasized his words.

I was shivering and light-headed, but I managed to whisper an answer. 'Yes.'

He settled himself, then placed the palm of his right hand firmly over the wound in my belly and his left hand on my forehead. His hands felt warm, and I thought it was because I was cold with shock. His gaze turned inward and his strong, dark brows drew together as he concentrated. The touch of his hands grew warmer still and my skin seemed to tingle where they rested. The pain faded from my mind, and for a few moments, I looked clearly at him. I can see that picture of Callum even now, if I choose. He was bareheaded, and the late sun had moved around to touch him, haloing his dark hair like that of a saint in a bible picture. Just for a moment, I felt that he was linked to the sun and the trees, drawing power from them and using himself to channel it through to me. Then I felt overwhelmingly drowsy, and the comforting

14

warmth of Callum's hands is the last thing I remember of that day.

It was dark when I woke again. I was wrapped warmly in a bedroll that smelt of someone else. A small campfire crackled nearby, its flames half-illuminating a dark-haired man sitting cross-legged and gazing into it. I remembered him kneeling beside me earlier, and just as I realized I wasn't in pain any more, I remembered the rustlers and my brother's body being dragged behind his horse.

'Abe!' I cried his name without meaning to, then turned my head to let my rolled-up coat absorb the tears that crowded out of my eyes. The grief swelled over me and I choked on it. When I had fought it down again, the stranger was beside me, holding out a tin cup, half full of water. I took it and drank gratefully.

'Thank you.' I handed the cup back to him. 'I guess I owe you my life. I'm Don Manor. I work for the Bar S.'

'Callum McGeachin,' he answered simply. 'Ah was riding along when Ah found youse lying in the grass. If Ah hadna' done something, ye'd be talkin' to Saint Peter be now.'

It was the longest sentence I'd heard from him, and it took me a few moments to make sense of his heavy accent. I was clearer in my mind now, and I studied him curiously as he spoke. Callum wore a

heavy black frockcoat over a white shirt and blue
Levis. I could just make out a black gunbelt underneath, with a short-barrelled Colt on one side, and
a spear-pointed knife on the other. A dark red ban-
danna was tied loosely around his neck, which with
his shaggy hair, gave him a faintly roguish look. A
gold ring on the little finger of his left hand
glinted in the firelight. His comfortably worn,
high-heeled riding boots seemed to have something missing, and it took me a few moments to
realize that Callum did not wear spurs. For the first
time I noticed that he was a smallish man, maybe
five foot four, compactly muscular, and slim of
waist. His personality was such that most of the
time I felt I was looking up at him. Only now and
again, seeing him at a distance with other people
around, would I remember what a small body he
inhabited.

At that moment, I was more puzzled by how he
had healed me, for I felt much stronger and yet
there didn't even seem to be any bandages over my
stomach.

'What did you do?' I asked. 'How did you save
my life?'

'That, laddie, Ah honestly canna explain t'ye.'
Callum's face suddenly widened into an impish
grin, revealing a slight gap between his front teeth.
'Ah want tae ken how ye got intae such a mess.'

I couldn't help warming to Callum's smile. In a

16

few minutes I told him what had happened that morning, and I wasn't ashamed of my tears when I told him about Abe's death. Callum was sympathetic, nodding solemnly as I talked.

'It's too late tae move now, an' ye need tae rest a wee while more,' he said. 'But tomorrer we'll gang tae look fer yer brother's body.'

'Thank you.' Callum's offer of help was a comfort to me, weak and grieving as I was. So it was that I lost my brother, Abe, and met Callum McGeachin, who was to be brother and more, in the short time we shared.

CHAPTER TWO

When I first woke the next morning, I thought that maybe I had dreamed Abe's death and all that had followed. But as soon as the sleep cleared from my head and I saw Callum cooking breakfast over a small fire, I knew my memory was true. What was hardest to believe was how close I'd come to death the day before. I sat up without discomfort and looked at my belly: the only sign of any injury was a new, pink scar. The flannel undershirt I wore, however, was stiff with dried blood, as were most of my clothes. A dark red shirt, not new but reasonably clean, lay on the bedroll.

'Ah'm no' certain how well it'll fit ye, laddie, but ye're welcome to ha' the use o' it,' Callum called.

I thanked him and tried the shirt on, moved by his generosity. Callum had spent the cold night wrapped in his coat and the two saddle blankets, while I slept in his bedroll. Now he was sharing his food and his clothes with me, a stranger. The shirt was a little too small, but I wore it in preference to my own. In the early morning light, I realized he was older than I'd first thought. I guessed now he was nearer forty than thirty, but that thick black hair and his trim build took years off him. Most of all it was his vitality that made him ageless.

As I ate bacon and fried potatoes, my thoughts kept turning to the mystery of how Callum had healed me. It occurred to me that he had evaded the question the night before. I owed him a lot, and didn't want to push in where I wasn't welcome, but my curiosity grew too strong. I finally spoke up while we were sipping coffee.

'Callum.' I spoke warily, uncertain of his reaction. 'I know you did something . . . miraculous last night. What power is it you have?'

He studied me for a minute, slow to commit himself to an answer. 'Ah'm a healer,' he said eventually. 'Ah ha' a gift in ma hands. Ah wasna' lyin' when Ah told ye Ah couldna' explain it. No one can explain it. There's a power runs in ma family, an' it's strong in me. Ah can use ma power tae heal.'

It sounded impossible, but Callum spoke matter of factly about it. Not only had I experienced proof myself of his gift, I could sense a power in him I'd never felt in anyone else. Whatever abilities Callum had, they were new and unknown to me,

19

and frightening. What could he use his power for, besides healing? As I sat and thought, I saw that Callum was watching me, waiting for my reaction. Now he was the wary one, not afraid of me, but ready to defend himself if necessary. My feelings changed at that moment, as he waited anxiously for my verdict on him. Callum's honesty, and his kindness to me, won over the fear.

I smiled, and he smiled happily in return.

'Right now, I'm damn glad you have your gift,' I told him.

'Ah'd rather ye didn't tell anyone about it,' Callum said, becoming serious again. 'Ye'll no' be fully strong yet, so ye maun tell yer boss ye've been hurt, but dinna let on how bad it was.'

I promised to keep his secret, and we were friends.

Callum and I arrived at the Bar S early that same afternoon. He was leading Abe's grey horse; Abe's body, wrapped in Callum's blanket, was tied across its fancy carved saddle. I was tired from riding and from weeping. Finding Abe's cold, battered body had been the moment when I really knew I had lost my brother forever. Callum had helped me straighten Abe's body and wrap it, then he held me as I cried for my loss. His quiet sympathy and my bitter tears gradually eased the raw pain, and my heart began the slow process of healing.

Ben Harmon saw us riding up and ran on to the ranch house to pass on the news. I led Callum past the corrals, where Ben had been working, and round the side of the two-storey ranch house to the yard out back. The yard area was enclosed by the bunk house and its cook house, the barns where hay and feed were stored, and the big building that was stable, cow shed and harness room, all under one roof. Young Joe Selby's black and white dog ran out from the stable to greet us, barking a welcome.

'Don!' Bibs Selby came hurrying from the lean-to door back of the ranch house. 'We were gettin' plumb worried about you.'

I sat astride Luke, too weary to dismount, and saw Selby take in the wrapped shape fastened to Abe's saddle. Selby hooked his thumbs into the bib of the old overalls he favoured, and looked from me to Callum. I shook my feet clear of my stirrups and let myself slide from the saddle, holding on to it for support. Slowly, I told Selby what had happened the day before. I didn't tell him how bad my wound had been, though there was plenty of dried blood on my trousers and my coat.

Selby frowned, and raised his hat to run one hand over his balding head.

'I'm real sorry, Don. Abe was a good man. I'll send Ben into Delta to fetch the preacher, and telegraph the sheriff too. Damn rustlers.' Selby paused, rubbing his head and thinking. After a few moments, he lowered his hat and looked up at Callum, who was still mounted. 'Thank you for helping Don. You're welcome to stay here a spell.'

'That's verra kind o' ye,' Callum answered. His expression changed from solemn to a smile in a moment, lighting him up. 'Ah'm no gang anywhere in particular at the moment,' he went on. 'An' Ah couldna help seeing youse got a corral of young horses here. Ah'm guid at gentlin' horses.'

'Ben usually breaks the young horses,' Selby answered slowly. He looked at me, seeing the pain I was in. 'I guess Don's not going to be fit to ride out for a few days. Ben would have to do his work anyway.'

Wrapped in my grief for Abe, I hadn't thought that Callum had no reason to stay at the Bar S. I got on well enough with the other hands here, but Abe and I had been so close I'd not needed to make proper friends before. I was suddenly afraid of Callum moving on and leaving me alone. I wanted him around, a friend to help heal my grief for my brother. And I was drawn to that mysterious power he had. I held my breath as I waited for Selby to reach his slow decision.

'All right,' Selby said at last. 'Just a half dozen of them; ten dollars a head, for each one that's good and saddle broke.'

Callum dismounted in a quick, graceful move,

and held out his hand. The deal was made and I breathed a sigh of relief.

My brother, Abraham Manor, was buried in a grassy meadow overlooking the Bar S. Everyone from the ranch attended: Selby, his wife and son, the other five hands, and Callum. The cold wind buffeted us as the preacher read from the Bible, and snatched his voice away. I'd written our parents with the news, and sent back most of Abe's belongings. I was relieved when the burial was over. No one knew what to say to me, and I lingered by the grave, looking at it and thinking of the men who had killed my brother. My grief began to turn to a festering anger. Those rustlers had no right to take my brother's life. Justice demanded that they pay for what they had done to Abe, and to me. I wanted revenge.

The sheriff came to see me, and once again I brought up the memories of that morning. I described the rustlers as best I could remember, 'They were changing the brand to the Circle HS,' I told him. 'Do you know that ranch?'

Sheriff Raynor shook his head. 'That's not a brand used anywhere in San Juan county, and I don't recall hearing of it elsewhere.' He didn't seem much interested.

'They murdered my brother,' I said hotly.

'Any cow thieves I round up, I'll let you know,'

Sheriff Raynor promised. 'You can come along and take a look; see if they're the ones.'

And that was the best he could offer me.

I wasn't strong enough to ride out on my regular duties of cow chasing. Selby set me to doing some chores around the yard, and mending ropes and horse harness, ready for the spring round-up. It was still cold, but when there was some sun, I liked to sit by the corrals and watch Callum gentling the young ponies, while I cleaned leather and braided ropes. The ponies were a bunch of wild youngsters we'd rounded up a few weeks earlier, when they were poor and hungry after the worst of the winter. They'd gotten used to the sights and sounds of the ranch, and to having hay pitched to them, but none of them was so much as halter-broke.

I was astonished the first time I watched Callum handle one of the broncs. He neatly roped a grey with a big white face, and got it into the smaller corral on its own. I expected him to get it running round and round to wear it out some before throwing a saddle on, but he did no such thing. He tied the grey short to the snubbing post in the centre of the corral, then backed off a couple of paces. The grey moved back as far as the rope would let it, and watched him like he was a cougar about to spring. Callum put his hands together behind his back, and slowly walked towards that pony. He leaned towards it, and at first, I couldn't make out what he was doing. Then I realised he was breathing gustily through his nose at the grey. The pony's ears pricked forward and it took a step closer to him. I swear that wild pony reached out with its muzzle and blew right back at him, like it would to another horse.

Callum was soon rubbing it behind the ears, and that grey pony stood there hip-shot, its eyes half closed as he talked softly to it. He had a halter tied round his waist, and soon he was fixing it over the grey's head. Then he stroked and touched that pony all over, running his hand down its legs and under its belly. That grey mustang acted as quiet as an old buggy horse. In less than an hour, Callum had it saddled and bridled, and was riding it around the corral. By the end of the day, it would walk, jog or lope as he told it, and turn neatly to a light touch on the reins. There was no bucking or the rough-riding that usually goes into 'breaking' wild ponies. Callum spoke truly when he said he 'gentled' them.

Outwardly, it seemed that little had changed at the Bar S. I didn't like the idea of Abe's bunk staying empty, reminding me of his absence, so I suggested Callum take it. He got on fine with the other hands, joining in the evening games of low stakes poker, and listening with the others when I read aloud from a book. I heard him singing one time, as he was grooming his bay mustang, and got him to sing in the bunkhouse that night. When he sang, his voice was strong and passionate, sometimes rough-edged and sometimes smooth. He sang ballads, sea shanties and drinking songs, and then some Scottish songs.

The last one was a plaintive piece, sung in a strange language. The soft glow of the oil lamp cast a pool of warmth in the dark bunkhouse. The mundane details of the room were in shadow as Callum's voice transported us to another country. I tore my gaze away from his face, and looked around at the other men, half-lit by the yellow flame. All were watching Callum; even Ben Harmon had forgotten his grievance over losing the job of breaking the wild ponies. His face was as rapt as the others, as Callum sang to us of loneliness and sorrow in the unfamiliar sounds of Gaelic. Callum's gaze was on the flame of the lamp, which reflected in miniature in his dark eyes. For a moment, I saw him again as I'd first seen him in the late afternoon sun, as he healed me. I felt he was somehow drawing strength from the lamp flame as he wove his spell with his voice. The song finished, and Callum looked into my eyes. I couldn't tell what he was thinking but he seemed to be satisfied with what he saw in me, for he smiled suddenly, and broke the spell of wonder.

*

A bare week after Abe's death, I felt fit enough to take up my riding duties again. Selby partnered me up with Ben, and told me to ride one of the ponies that Callum had gentled. I chose the grey with the white face and spoke quiet to it. The grey pricked its ears at me, and stood patient as I heaved up the girths and made them tight. Ben was saddling his sorrel, a horse that he'd broken through rough riding a couple of years earlier. Selby watched me as I lifted up the grey's feet to pick them out.

'Callum sure seems to have some touch with those ponies,' Selby remarked. He moved closer and patted the grey on the neck; it didn't flinch or shy away.

I scraped a wad of dirt from the sole of the grey's near hind. 'It's not just him they trust,' I said. 'A child could handle them.'

Ben snorted loudly. 'Why, you don't know that. Ain't none of them hosses been ridden outside the corral yet. Those mustangs ain't broke proper. If you don't ride 'em down an' show them who's boss, how do you know they ain't gonna play you up?'

'What about the time that pinto you broke blew up on a mountain trail and dumped you over the edge?' I reminded him. 'You slid twenty feet afore you got stopped by a pine tree. You were picking needles outta your butt for days.'

Ben flushed with anger, chewing on the long ends of his moustache, as he tried to find an answer.

'Quit your yapping and get yourselves out and looking after my beef,' Selby ordered us. He looked at me. 'Take it gently today, Don. If the grey gives you too much trouble, head on back and get one from your string.'

I nodded, and swung myself into the saddle. The grey answered to a light touch on the rein, walking out well as Ben and I followed the trail away from the Bar S.

We rode in silence at first. I was concentrating on the grey pony; its ears were pricked and I could feel its excitement at leaving the familiar ranch surroundings. I spoke to the pony, and stroked its mane. Ben's snort of disapproval was loud. We rode on aways, both bundled up against the chilly air. The sky was overcast, promising rain later. The peaks to the south were wrapped in mufflers of cloud. My enjoyment at being out again was broken by Ben's voice.

'I guess you didn't hear anything from the sheriff yet?' he asked. Something in the tone of his voice needled me. I glanced at him, disliking his bulging, pale blue eyes and his flat face. He sat heavily in his saddle, keeping a good hold on his reins as his horse tugged against the unnecessary pressure on its bit.

'Not yet,' I answered.

'And not likely to,' Ben said. He shook his head. 'I'd be mad as all hell iffen someone murdered my brother.'

I felt my face warm with a flush of anger. 'And you think I'm not? You think I've forgotten about Abe?'

Ben looked at me, his pale eyes insolent. 'Well, what are you doin' about it? You saw the men who killed your brother; when are you goin' to go look for them?'

My jaw clenched tight with anger as his words hit home. In the quiet of the last few days, I'd been thinking about Abe's murder, and the men who'd killed him. A part of me called out for revenge; to go out and find the rustlers. To shoot them like they'd shot Abe. They'd killed my younger brother and it burned in me that it was right that I should see justice done. Another part of myself kept putting up objections. I couldn't go look for the rustlers without quitting my job, and with spring coming, the Bar S needed all its hands. And how was I, no gunman, to take on three or more outlaws? Most of all, I had no idea how to track down three men who could be almost anyplace in one large state, if they were still in Colorado at all. Surely the sheriff was better fitted to find the rustlers than I was?

'We got law in this state,' I told Ben. 'If everyone

upped and went off to do justice like they saw fit, innocent folks would get killed and there wouldn't be no peace anywhere.'

Ben's answer was a scornful look; he wasn't fooled for a moment. I thought he was going to challenge me some more, but he dug his spurs into his horse's sides, and urged it into a gallop.

'Come on, Don,' he called. 'Let's see iffen Callum broke that horse enough for you to race it.'

The grey was plunging excitedly, so I released the reins and let it gallop. It was easier to think about riding than to think about my brother.

CHAPTER THREE

All those wild ponies that Callum gentled turned
out well. Bibs Selby was as pleased as a pup with a
new collar. Unbroken, the mustangs were worth
about two dollars a head. Ones busted by rough
riding methods fetched around twenty dollars, and
could be guaranteed to buck a few times whenever
saddled. When Callum had finished with his
ponies, they were quiet enough for women to ride,
and could be sold for thirty to forty dollars each.
Selby was loud in his praise, and bought five mustangs cheap off another rancher, who hadn't yet
gotten around to breaking them.

Ben Harmon was the only one who didn't like
the way things were going. He was mad at missing
out on the money he usually got for breaking
broncs. If Callum had bragged on his skill at gentling the ponies, we might have taken Ben's side,
but Callum made no fuss about his talent. So far as

31

he was concerned, he was working with the horses in the way he thought best, and if he produced results that suited other folk, so much the better. Ben took a fancy to one of the new mustangs, a stocky roan, and asked Selby if he could have it for his string. I guess Selby was feeling some guilty about Ben not having the chance to earn his bronc money, and he agreed.

Ben asked for his horse on a Sunday afternoon, when we were pretty free from work until the evening chores needed doing. I was sitting outside the bunk house, reading a magazine story aloud to Chickenwings, Sawtooth and Hank. Earl was inside, snoring, and Callum had taken his own mount out to stretch its legs. Ben swaggered over to us and stood casual, one thumb hooked into the waistband of his brown ribbed trousers.

'Ole Selby done give me that roan for my string,' he announced, interrupting my reading. 'I aim to see it gets broken proper. A hoss needs to know who's master.' He grinned in a way I didn't like, and walked on over to the stable.

I started up reading again, but had just finished the page when Ben came out of the stable carrying his saddle and bridle. He took no notice of us, but walked briskly across the yard, aiming for the corrals by the ranch house. I closed the magazine and called after him.

'Ben? You ain't going to start riding the roan

now, are you?'

'Why not?' He didn't slow down, barely even turned as he answered. 'Selby put the pony in my string, and I've busted plenty of broncs before now.'

I got hurriedly to my feet, and ran across the yard after Ben. The others flocked behind me, eager to see what would happen. Ben slung his saddle on the top rail of the small corral and turned to face me.

'This one ain't Callum's job,' he growled. 'It's in my string, and I'll handle it the way I want. I'm gonna show you all a real bronc buster at work.'

I didn't know how to argue with him. Going behind Callum's back was an insult, but that's what Ben intended.

Ben neatly roped the roan and got it into the small corral. He flipped the end of his rope at it, and got that pony running round and around the corral, until its coat was dark with sweat. Every time it started to slow, Ben yelled at it and hazed it on some more. Only when it was tuckered out, did he tie it to the snubbing post. The roan laid back its ears, showing the whites of its eyes as it watched Ben warily. Ben wasn't all hot air; he knew how to handle mustangs and soon had that roan cross-hobbled with a length of grass rope. With one hind leg tied up in the air, that pony couldn't do no more than snort and hop around as Ben got the bridle on. He took his time fixing the saddle, heaving the girths up good and tight.

'I bet five bucks I don't hit the dirt more'n once,' he bragged, slapping the roan on the shoulder.

'Five bucks says it's twice,' Chickenwings called, blinking in his slow way.

'I'll lay on three times,' Earl offered.

Ben was grinning fit to bust, and I suddenly saw how much he enjoyed being the centre of attention. 'Hold on to your hats, boys,' he called. 'I'm gonna bust him loose.' He quickly released the rope hobbles, then grasped the roan's ear, twisting it to distract the pony as he climbed aboard. In a moment, his feet were home in the stirrups and he let go the pony's ear.

The mustang bounded forward, humping its back. Ben whooped as it leaped across the corral on stiff legs, jarring him hard every time it hit the ground. At the far side of the corral, the roan reared, pawing at the sky with its front hoofs. Ben leaned forward, and punched it between the ears to bring it down again. The mustang snorted and set off again in large, twisting bucks. I knew myself that those could be the devil to sit, but Ben hardly moved in his saddle. His hat had slid off and was hanging on his shoulders by its strap, bouncing every time the horse left the ground. The other hands cheered him on as the mustang spun in a tight circle, then got its head down and kicked for the sky. I heard Ben grunt as the saddlehorn dug into his guts, but he was still aboard as the roan took off in a series of long leaps. The mustang's legs and belly were coated in reddish dirt it had kicked up in its frantic fight, and its sweat had worked into a white froth under its saddle. We were all watching the struggle between man and horse, too absorbed to see or hear Callum approaching.

The first I knew was when a rope flew out from beside me, and landed around the roan's neck. I turned my head and saw Callum, dallying his rope around the top of a corral post. He was watching Ben and the roan, his face set in tight lines of fury. The roan tried to leap away but the rope brought it up short and it fell to its knees.

Chickenwings and Earl were yelling, but I was between them and Callum as he climbed swiftly over the logs of the corral fence, and dropped lightly down inside.

'Get your Goddam rope off of my horse!' Ben yelled, as the roan lurched back to its feet. It stood with its head low, sobbing for breath.

Callum had one hand on his rope, and I took hold of the dally, elbowing Earl back.

'It's between them two,' I said, giving him a look that dared him to disagree.

Callum was walking slowly towards Ben, his

movements deliberate. I couldn't see his face but I could feel his fury, feeding from that power he carried within himself.

'Get off ma horse now,' Callum demanded, his voice low and clear.

Ben reached forward to loosen the rope from the roan's neck. 'Selby gave me this pony for my string.'

Callum had reached him and stood looking up. 'Ah said, get off ma horse.'

'It's not your horse.' Ben pulled the loosened rope forwards, to drop it over the roan's ears. He was leaning over the pony's neck, his shirt brushing its sweaty, black mane.

Callum's hands shot out. He grabbed a double handful of Ben's blue shirt and hauled him roughly from the saddle. Ben managed to kick his feet clear as he came off, landing hard on his rump and rolling over.

'I'll no' stand by an' see ye ride that wee horse like you was the Devil himsel'!' Callum hissed. 'There's nae need tae break his spirit, damn youse!'

At that moment, Callum himself looked more like the devil, with his wild black hair, and fury glowing in his eyes.

Ben rolled himself onto his knees and scrambled up. 'Go to the devil yourself!' he yelled, throwing himself at Callum.

36

Callum swung out of his way, ramming hard fists into Ben's body. Ben turned with the impact, swinging a backhanded blow that caught Callum on the ear. It put Callum off balance just long enough for Ben to finish turning and face him. Ben deflected a punch aimed for his face, and jabbed out in return, missing as Callum ducked. The roan pony retreated to the other side of the corral and watched the fight fearfully. Callum and Ben traded blows for some minutes, grunting when fists landed. Ben had the advantage of reach and youth, but Callum was clearly an experienced fighter. He would duck inside Ben's blows and jab both fists into Ben's belly before breaking clear again. As we watched, the other hands yelling encouragement indiscriminately, it looked as though Callum was slowly getting the best of the fight. In desperation, Ben lunged forward, taking advantage of his longer reach to grab Callum's frock coat. Callum reacted instantly, seizing hold of Ben's arms to brace himself as he kicked.

The pointed toe of his boot hit Ben on the kneecap, bringing a yell of pain. Ben lurched to one side, still holding on to Callum. His weight pulled Callum off balance, and Ben used that to throw Callum to the ground. Callum landed rolling, fetching up close to the frightened roan pony. It whinnied and laid its ears back. I yelled a warning, but I doubt if Callum heard me. He was scrambling to his feet, hampered briefly by the skirt of his muddy coat. Ben had managed to stay on his feet, and now he ran towards Callum, fists raised. Callum took a step backwards, wanting to give himself a moment longer to regain his balance. He got too close to the frightened roan pony. It squealed and lashed out with both hind legs.

I think I screamed something as Callum was kicked almost clear across the corral. I know I was already running around outside the corral as he hit the ground hard, rolled once, and slammed into one of the upright fence posts. A breathless cry of pain was forced from him as he hit the solid log, then he lay huddled and still. I reached him and dropped to my knees, calling his name. He moaned a little with each gasping breath. I reached between the corral rails to put my hand on his shoulder.

'Callum, how badly hurt are you?' I cried.

He rolled more on to his back, his coat twisted about him, and reached up to put his hand over mine, where it rested on his shoulder. The contact was startling, almost like an electric shock from a telegraph machine. Callum closed his eyes and drew in a slow, deep breath, then another. Colour returned to his face and when he opened his eyes again, they were bright and clear. He released my hand and looked at me, his dark eyes warm with gratitude. Carefully, he stood up, and turned to face Ben again. I leaned against the corral rails, shaken by the experience.

Sawtooth had climbed into the corral and caught the roan pony's reins. Earl and Hank were pulling, swinging the gate wide open to let him lead the frightened, sweaty animal out. Ben was on his feet, facing Callum, his face truculent. His look changed as Callum walked slowly and deliberately towards him, his fists raised. Ben glanced at the stout corral post Callum had slammed into, then looked at Callum again. I picked myself up, holding on to the corral rails for support, and moved around so I could see Callum's face. He was smeared with mud and bleeding from a graze on his right cheek, and a split lip, but his power shone from his eyes. The other men were standing still, watching him too. It was surely impossible that any man could recover so quickly from being kicked into a post by a mustang. The kick alone had been enough to break ribs and leave a man groaning in agony.

Fear crept into Ben's face as Callum came closer, moving steadily and easily. Ben half-lifted one hand, but his nerve had gone. Callum stopped beyond arm's reach of the other man.

'Ah told ye ah dinna like ma horses being rough-ridden,' Callum said, almost calmly. 'Ah doan hold wi' hurting other creatures.'

With that, he stepped forward and lashed around a punch that took Ben Harmon on the jaw. Ben shot backwards and measured his length on the ground. Callum stared down at him for a moment, then moved towards the corral gate to take the horse.

'Callum!' I circled around the corral towards him, forgetting my momentary weakness after his accident. 'I'll see to the pony. You take care of yourself.'

He stopped, and ran his fingers through his sweat-streaked hair. Then his face broke into a sudden, impish smile. 'Thank ye, Don. Ah'm grateful.'

Callum set off for the bunkhouse, and I went to take the roan. Sawtooth was watching Callum walk away, his face thoughtful. As I took the reins, he looked at me and said:

'There's something plumb uncanny about that man. Unnatural.'

I didn't like the undertone of fear in his voice, but I couldn't disagree.

I led that little roan horse to the stable and took my time over caring for it. Of course I was worried about Callum, but he'd given so much of himself in his concern for the horse, and then trusted me to finish the job. The tired roan made no fuss as I led it into a box stall, and removed the saddle and bridle. I gave it water, then set in to currying it from nose to tail. I brushed every last bit of mud and sweat off its chestnut and white flecked coat, talking nonsense quietly to it as I worked. After a while, the roan began to twitch its ear back to listen to me. I left that horse standing deep in golden straw, clean, and pulling sweet hay from its rack. It had learnt that man could bring comfort as well as pain and fear. I was satisfied.

Callum was in the yard, sitting against the wall of the cookhouse in a patch of late afternoon sunlight. There was little warmth in the sun, so soon after winter, but Callum had his face turned to it, absorbing it just as he took in warmth from the coffee mug he held in his small, square hands. The light burnished his black hair and betrayed the lines of weariness in his face. He had cleaned himself up and changed his clothes, but the improvement was only on the surface. As I approached, he shifted position slightly, stiff and wincing with pain.

'How's the wee horse?' Callum asked as I sat down beside him.

'Calm now, I reckon he'll do fine,' I answered. 'He looks better than you do.'

Callum leaned against me, giving an involuntary gasp of pain as he moved. He stayed still for a few moments, breathing shallowly, before relaxing again. 'Between the horse an' the post, Ah reckon Ah've got ribs broke all round,' he said softly.

41

'Can't you ... help, yourself?' I asked quietly. 'Like you did for me?'

Callum shook his head, keeping the movement small. 'Ah can use an' direct ma power but, for guid nor ill, Ah canna use it on mahself, not directly.' He spoke straightforwardly, discussing his strange gifts without shame, fear or pride. 'Ah can draw strength frae other things tae keep me goin' while Ah heal up, an' tae heal faster, but Ah canna work miracles on mahsel'.'

He finished up his coffee, then leaned his head against my shoulder.

'Sawtooth said there was something uncanny about you,' I told him.

'Uncanny?' Callum repeated softly. 'Aye, he's right enough.'

We sat together without talking. Hens bustled about the yard, seeking grain. A ginger cat appeared from the stables with a mouse grasped in its teeth, and ran in long leaps to the barn. I could hear voices in the bunkhouse, now and again, and then the rattling of cast-iron pans in the cook-house behind us as Chickenwings started fixing supper. I think Callum slept for a while, there in the sunshine. He rested against me like a tired child, exhausted from the effort needed to get back on his feet again after being kicked across the corral. I slowly got the sense of his strength return-ing, the strength he needed to draw on until his

42

injuries healed.

When Chickenwings rang the bell to call everyone for supper, the sun had gone behind the crests of the mountains. Callum stirred and sat up, moving without evident pain. His dark eyes were bright as he lifted his head and sniffed the air.

'Och, Ah'm so hungry,' he said with feeling. 'That stew smells guid enough fer a king.' He scrambled up, wincing a little as he straightened, then smiled. I found I was cold and hungry too, and a little shaky as I climbed to my feet.

'Come on, Don.' Callum clapped me on the shoulder. 'Let's go an' eat. A girt, strong laddie like youse needs his food.'

He headed for the cookhouse door, and I followed him, that small, uncanny, warm-hearted man.

CHAPTER FOUR

Bibs Selby soon enough learned about the fight, and spoke privately to both Ben and Callum. I never knew exactly what was said, but the upshot was that Ben was told to choose a horse that Callum had already gentled, and Callum was to have complete charge of the roan, and the other unbroken horses.

I don't think anyone else ever realized how bad Callum's injuries had been. He did his work, ate all the food offered, and slept from supper till breakfast, restoring the inner strength he needed to conceal his pain. Although he couldn't heal himself as he did others, I learned that he recovered from injury remarkably fast. A week after the fight, Callum was as healthy as when I first met him.

Ben didn't have the guts to challenge Callum again after their fight. Instead he took out his resentment on me, needling me with nasty remarks when there was no one else to hear. He knew I was too proud to tell Callum about it. I'd have to stand up to him myself, or else prove Ben right when he accused me of not having the guts to solve my own problems. I did my best to ignore him, and to avoid being alone with Ben, but his words festered inside me.

Calving season was upon us. The time for horse-breaking was past, and Callum rode out with us as we watched over the cows. Spring was taking over from winter, though we helped deliver a few calves in snowstorms. The aspens in the lower valleys began to show delicate green, and the breeze carried the songs of chickadees and warblers as they competed for territories, and for mates. But I couldn't enjoy myself, with Ben's continuous slow drip of accusation and spite. I'm sure Callum guessed that something was wrong, but he didn't press me about it. I stayed quiet, bottling up my resentment for as long as I could.

Things boiled over at the end of calving season. Shelby had told me and Ben to work together one day, and I hadn't any good reason to refuse. All that day, as we rode after cows and calves, I expected Ben to start into making his comments. But he didn't say anything more than he had to. I couldn't believe that he'd quit trying to get at me, and I was waiting for him to start. All through the day I was waiting, getting nervier as the sun moved round and it got towards suppertime. Now and then, I caught him looking at me with those bulgy eyes of his, and smiling to himself. It made me as jumpy as a long-tailed cat in a room full of rocking chairs.

It was when we were riding back home that Ben started talking. He waited until we were in clear sight of the corrals and said casually.

'You know what McGeachin aims to spend his hoss-breaking money on?'

I shook my head. 'Nope.'

'Whiskey an' whores, I expect,' Ben said edging his horse close to mine. 'I bet he can buy himself a fine piece of tail with what Selby's done paid him.'

I didn't like to hear Ben guessing about Callum that way, but tried not to show it as I answered, 'It's no business of mine what Callum spends his money on.'

Ben thought for a moment before speaking again. 'I wonder what sort of woman he goes for? A nice plump one you can lose yourself in? Blondes?'

'I don't give a damn!' I snapped, my edgy mood getting the better of me.

Ben grinned at me nastily. 'What you making such a fuss about, Don? Don't you like to think about Callum goin' with a woman when you want him all to yourself?'

I simply stared at Ben for a moment, taken aback by his suggestion. Then I lost my temper completely.

I launched myself from my saddle at Ben, grabbing him around the shoulders. My weight dragged Ben from his saddle and we hit the ground together, fighting. We rolled over and over, throwing wild punches and curses. I was so furious I hardly felt Ben's blows. I managed to get atop him, and lashed hard punches into his face, trying to obliterate the memory of his nasty smile. Ben grabbed the front of my coat and hauled me down, bringing up his head fast. The top of his head smashed against my mouth, splitting my lips against my teeth.

He immediately shoved me backwards, rolling me over and pinning me down. His knee landed in my stomach, winding me. I was struggling to breathe, helpless for a few moments as Ben laid into me. Then I got my breath back in a sudden heave of aching lungs. Fired with new strength and anger, I brought my legs up to ram my knees into Ben's back. Ben lurched forward and I lashed out with a straight, hard punch. It hit right on his jaw, snapping his head back. I got my feet on the ground again and arched my back, throwing Ben from me.

Without thinking about what I was doing, I half stood, then dropped on Ben, landing with both knees on his stomach. The breath was forced from him in a harsh grunt. As he lay, writhing and gasping, I rained punch after punch on to his face. I wasn't thinking any more, but as long as he was there in front of me, I hit him. Blood was smeared across his face, staining his moustache. I hardly knew how much damage I was doing to him. All I wanted to do was pummel him.

Hands grabbed me under the arms and hauled me away.

'That's enough now, laddie.'

I recognized Callum's voice and stopped struggling. Callum and Selby had hold of me; Sawtooth was leaning over Ben, who was barely conscious. My breathing slowed as the fury left me, and I became aware of pain, and the taste of blood in my mouth. As I relaxed, Bibs Selby let go of me. Callum kept hold, supporting me as I recovered. Selby took his hat off and ran his hand over his balding head before speaking.

'What happened, Don? What made you straighten Ben's plough?' Selby looked puzzled and disappointed.

I took a deep breath before answering. 'I didn't like something he said.' It wasn't much of a defence, but I didn't want to tell everything.

Selby looked at me long and hard. 'Was it something about Abe?' he asked.

I was tempted to answer yes, but honesty won

out and I shook my head.

'You've never been one to go off half-cocked, Don,' Selby said slowly. 'But I won't stand for my hands brawling like this. I'll speak to Ben about this later, when he's fit to talk. Meantime, you can see to his horse as well as your own, and get yourself cleaned up some.'

'Sure, boss,' I answered dispiritedly, and did as he said.

After supper, I went outside to sit on the top rail of the corral. My body was bruised and sore, but I felt worse inside. I didn't much regret beating up on Ben, but I knew our fight would only make things worse. Ben wasn't the sort to forgive, and the other hands no longer knew what to think of me. We'd got on fine in the past, but Abe had always been there as my closest company. I was a dreamer, the reader of stories; I was just different enough to make my friendship with the other hands fragile. Attacking Ben for reasons I couldn't explain had made them wary.

I'd been on my own for about half an hour when Callum came to join me. We gazed at the mountains awhile, watching as the pink blush of sunset coloured the snow. Behind us, the horses in the corral settled down, blowing out occasional, gusty sighs. At length, Callum stirred, and turned to look at me.

'Ah'm ready tae move on,' he said. There was a

49

question in his dark eyes.

I nodded slowly. 'I hate to quit this close to spring roundup, but. . . .' It was the question I'd been debating with myself for weeks. I didn't want to leave the ranch short-handed, especially as Callum would be leaving too. I felt bad enough tonight already.

Callum seemed to know what I was thinking. 'There'll no' be a guid time tae leave,' he said. 'Ye can always find a reason tae stay if ye want one.'

I gazed towards the mountains, now silhouetted against the last light of the day. For a little longer I struggled with the decision, thinking of Abe, of Callum, of this ranch where I had lived and worked.

'I don't want it to look like I'm running away,' I said at last. 'I'm not scared of Ben, but it don't seem worth staying here any more. Every chance he gets, he's saying things, trying to make me mad.'

'He went an' succeeded the day,' Callum remarked drily.

I half-smiled at that. 'I can't promise Selby it won't happen again.' I paused and then said. 'Tomorrow morning, I'll tell Selby I want to leave.'

Callum grinned suddenly. 'Ah'll be glad tae ha' ye wi' me.'

I grinned back, lighter in heart now the decision was made.

Two days later, on a fine spring morning that smelled of hope and growing things, Callum and I rode away from the Bar S.

'Nowhere to go, and plenty of time to get there,' I said happily. The horses seemed to pick up our mood as we jogged along the grassy upland meadow. Callum's bay mustang threw three bucks for the joy of being alive on such a day. Callum laughed, sitting the bucks easily, and called his horse a fool.

'Was there anywhere you wanted to go?' I asked, not having given much thought to the practicality of moving on.

'Ah hear there's hot springs over tae Ouray,' Callum said, rolling his rrr's thoroughly as he said the town's name. 'After all the work we've done wi' them cows, Ah reckon we've earned ourselves a guid soak.' His gap-toothed grin turned impish. 'An' it's no' far frae Ouray tae Silverton, an' Ah've heard Silverton's the place for saloons an' wimmin; some verra good, bad wimmin, if ye ken me?'

By this time, I'd grown used to Callum's Scottish accent, and I did indeed understand what he meant. I grinned back, and we rode on.

Those few days of freedom were bright and happy ones. We headed south along the Uncompahgre river, enjoying the changing scenery as the saw-toothed mountains got larger and closer in that sweet, pure air. We didn't bother to stop in Montrose, but when we reached Ridgeway two days later, the smell coming from the restaurant was too much to resist after a week of trail cooking.

'Ma treat,' Callum said, smiling, as we hitched our horses outside the long, low building.

'It'll surely be a treat not to be eating my own cooking,' I answered cheerfully.

The restaurant was a decently clean place that showed a woman's touch in the red checked table-cloths and a green glass vase of early wildflowers on the windowsill. We sat at a small table, not too far from a counter that had a tempting display of pies and cakes. I picked up one of the hand-written menus that were propped between the salt and pepper shakers, and offered one to Callum. He shook his head.

'Ah know what ah want. A guid piece of steak will do fer me.'

I glanced down the list as the waiter approached. 'They do chicken pie,' I commented. 'That's sounds good.'

Callum grinned. 'Och, I'll go wi' ye on that then.'

I gave the orders, then glanced through the window at the grassy land outside.

'It seems strange to be in a restaurant at

52

midday,' I said. 'Not out working. I feel like I got let out of school for an early vacation.'

'Ah know what ye mean,' Callum answered. 'Though ah dinna attend school verra much.' His expression changed as he thought back into his past. 'There was a lot of us bairns, an' ma parents couldna' afford the pennies to send all of us tae school.'

I suddenly understood why Callum hadn't taken a copy of the menu, and he saw that knowledge in my face.

'Ah canna read,' he admitted. 'At least, no' like youse. Ah know ma letters, an' Ah can write ma name,' he added with a touch of pride, and started to trace the letters with his forefinger, on the table-cloth.

Like many cowhands, I carried a stub pencil and a small notebook in my vest pocket. I offered them to Callum, who took them, adjusting his hold on the pencil awkwardly. I'd seen him use his hands to effortlessly throw ropes, tie knots and control horses. Now he laboured to write his own name in plain, childish letters: *Callum McGeachin.*

'Ah thought Ah was lucky then, no' goin' tae school,' Callum said. 'But Ah wish Ah'd had the chance, now. What was your school like?'

He kept me talking about my childhood until the food arrived, leaning forward with his elbows on the table and listening intently. I talked about

Abe, of course, and the memories were bitter sweet. It still seemed wrong that he had gone, but I was slowly adjusting to life without him around. There were still times when I saw something and thought to myself that I would tell Abe about it later. The pain hit me at those times, but now was the first time I'd been able to look back at our shared childhood, and enjoy the memories.

Ridgeway was a small town, and there wasn't much business in the restaurant. We were full of good, home-cooked food, and enjoying coffee, when a woman entered. I saw at a glance that she was a lady, not a woman of joy. She wore a tailored black coat over a full, blue divided skirt that swung as she walked towards the waiter. Dark hair was neatly pinned up under her hat and I saw blue eyes in her lovely, classical face. They were good clothes, not fussy, and she made no effort to draw attention to them or to herself. She was a born lady in every inch of her straight and shapely figure.

I heard a small sigh from Callum, and glanced across the table, to see him watching the woman with a look that mingled wonder and appreciation.

'Good afternoon, Mrs Molloy,' the waiter said. 'Can I help you?'

'Do you know where Doctor Reynolds is?' she asked, in a clear, educated voice.

'Ah now.' The waiter shook his head. 'He done

got called out to the Yankee Girl mine. A feller was takin' a ride back up on the aerial tramway and wasn't sitting low enough in the ore car. Bashed his head against one of the support towers, he did.'

'Oh, dear.' The news was a disappointment to her. Her face fell and the light died from her eyes.

'What did you want him for?' the waiter asked. scratching his balding head.

'My little girl, Sallie, she's got a bad fever,' Mrs Molloy said, her voice shaking slightly. 'I've been nursing her, but she's not improving.' She turned to glance impatiently towards the door, as if thinking about leaving. 'I can't ride after Doctor Reynolds,' she said, almost to herself. 'There's no one but Joey to look after Sallie.'

I heard Callum's chair scrape on the lumber floor, then he was up and walking across the room. He stopped a polite distance from Mrs Molloy, who was only a couple of inches shorter than he was, and nodded to her.

'Excuse me fer interruptin', but mebbe ah can help youse,' he offered. Her lovely face lit up. 'Oh! Could you ride to the Yankee Girl and find the doctor for me?' she asked.

'If ye wish so,' Callum answered. 'But Ah'm guid at healing folks mysel'. Ah'm sure it would be quicker if Ah came tae see your wee daughter.'

'That's a kind offer,' Mrs Molloy said slowly. She was looking more closely at Callum, now taking more notice of his shaggy hair and travel-stained clothes.

He understood what she was thinking, and suddenly produced that impish, gap-toothed grin. 'Ma name's Callum McGeachin. Me an' Don, we've been wurrkin' for the Bar S, but we took a fancy tae movin' on.'

Mrs Molloy followed Callum's glance in my direction, noticing me for the first time.

'Callum's telling the plumb truth about being good at curing folks,' I said. 'If anyone can help your daughter, he can.'

Mrs Molloy sighed softly, thinking things through. We didn't know it then, but to send someone to the mine and back would take the best part of two days, even if the doctor could come immediately. Mrs Molloy had to be grateful for whatever help was offered. She looked up at Callum and produced a faint smile. 'Thank you. I'll be glad of your help,' she told Callum.

I sometimes wonder how different things would have been if Anne Molloy hadn't decided to trust that small, black-haired Scotsman. None of us, not even Callum for all his gifts, knew what lay ahead.

CHAPTER FIVE

From Ridgeway, we followed Mrs Molloy south-
wards, with the Mount Sneffels range raising its
snow-glittering peaks ahead of us. Like most of the
range women out here, she rode astride, sitting
her grey saddle horse well as it climbed steadily. I
guess her mind was on her sick daughter, for she
wasn't inclined to talk. It was only when riding out
of Ridgeway that she had thought to introduce
herself to us fully.

'I'm Mrs Molloy,' she said, her attention more
on the trail ahead and her family waiting for her.
'Anne Molloy.'

Callum smiled. 'Anne. Now that's a name o'
queens an' saints.'

Anne Molloy looked a little startled at that, then
smiled properly for the first time since we'd seen
her.

There was little more conversation after that.

Callum asked the names of the peaks ahead of us, and Mrs Molloy pointed to them in turn. We rode for some two hours before she pointed to a little cluster of buildings set in the open ground at the bottom of the wood-sided valley we were following. The ranch house was a two-storey affair, solidly built of thick boards set on a stone foundation; a difference in the colour of the boards at front and back suggested it had been expanded at some time. Around it were the wagon shelter, stables, barn and smaller buildings like a chicken house and a root cellar. From a distance, it looked like a good set-up, but as we got closer, I began to notice signs of disrepair.

A lot of the fencing needed mending after winter damage, and shingles were missing from the stable roof. The truck garden behind the house needed digging over ready for the new sowing of vegetables. Two milk cows leaned against a rickety fence, bellowing to be milked, while their calves answered in long calls from the barn. The small flock of hens rushed to the kitchen door as it opened, hoping to be fed. A coltish boy of about nine, with a mop of thick brown hair, came out and waved to us.

'That's my son, Joey,' Mrs Molloy said, her voice anxious.

I was looking at a door on the stable that was sagging on its hinges. 'Is your husband out on the range?' I asked.

'Tom, my husband, died of pneumonia two years ago,' Mrs Molloy answered. 'The three men who were working for us stayed on a while, but they got offered better money elsewhere, and quit just before the winter set in.' She couldn't quite disguise the bitterness in her voice.

'So, ye've been all alone, then. You an' your bairns?' Callum asked sympathetically.

'We've managed so far,' Mrs Molloy answered stiffly.

Joey came out to meet us as we rode into the yard. He held his mother's horse as she dismounted, looking at me and Callum with unabashed curiosity.

'Sallie's awfully hot, and she won't sleep none,' Joey said to Mrs Molloy.

She produced a smile for him. 'These men have come to help her get better. Water the horses, Joey, and then milk poor Betsy and Blossom.'

'Sure, mom.' Joey took the reins of all three horses and led them across to a wooden trough.

We followed Mrs Molloy through the flock of flustering hens and into the kitchen. The ranch house was better kept up inside, clean and smelling of soap and baked goods. Braided rugs and framed samplers added colour to the kitchen, and a pile of snowy sheets awaited ironing. The cookstove gleamed with blacklead.

'Would you like coffee?' Mrs Molloy offered.

'No' just yet, thank ye,' Callum answered. 'Though it would be a guid idea tae put the kettle on tae heat.' He held up a small leather pouch he had taken from his saddle-bag. 'Ah reckon an infusion o' these herbs will be guid for yer daughter, but Ah'd like tae see her first.'

'Of course; follow me, please.'

Again, the same impression of modest, homely comfort could be glimpsed in the narrow hall between the kitchen and the parlour. Upstairs, I saw the doors to a largish bedroom over the parlour, and two smaller ones over the kitchen. The corridor extended along to the newer part of the house at the back.

'That's where the men slept,' Mrs Molloy told us, indicating the rear of the house. 'You're welcome to stay there tonight. There's another staircase that leads down to a room at the back, with its own door to the yard. Tom built it so they could come and go without disturbing us.'

'We'd be grateful for a place tae stay,' Callum said, following her into one of the smaller bedrooms.

The room was stuffy, and smelt of fever. Flowered calico curtains were pulled almost closed, leaving the room dim apart from the bright shafts of sunlight that spotlit swirling specks of dust. Mrs Molloy's daughter was in a small wooden bed, heaped with a bright patchwork quilt and fat feather pillows. Her hair was as dark as her mother's, done up in two long, loose braids to keep it off her neck and face.

'Momma!'

'Home already,' Mrs Molloy said cheerfully, bending to kiss Sallie on her cheek. 'Dr Reynolds is away, but these men have kindly come to help you get better.' She poured water from a flower-painted jug into a small cup, and held it for the little girl to drink.

I moved to the foot of the bed, not wanting to get in the way, or appear too threatening to the child. Callum stood by as Mrs Molloy plumped up the pillows and made Sallie comfortable, then he sat on the edge of the bed and smiled.

'You're a bonnie wee thing,' he said to Sallie. 'An' that's a pretty dolly there. What's her name?' He pointed to a rag doll tucked up beside Sallie. Sallie stared at Callum for a moment before speaking. 'Her name's Laura.'

'Has she been sick too?' Callum asked.

Sallie nodded. Callum sympathized, and in a few moments more he had won Sallie over completely. Mrs Molloy stood back and watched as Callum gently examined Sallie, looking at her eyes, feeling her forehead, and listening to her breathe, as he asked her questions about herself, her doll, and the animals on the ranch. When he was done,

Callum handed his leather pouch to Mrs Molloy.

'Two teaspoons infused in a mug o' hot water will help wi' this flu,' he said.

As soon as she had left the room, Callum asked me to pull back the curtains. Sunlight flooded in, making Sallie blink. Callum soaked in the light for a few moments then turned his attention back to the child.

'Now, rest and make yoursel' comfortable,' he said, taking her right hand in his own. 'Close your eyes an' think o' your favourite things.' He placed his left hand on her forehead, and began to concentrate, his dark brows drawing together.

I watched from near the window, fascinated, and unwilling to move in case I disturbed Callum and broke his spell of concentration. His lips moved slightly, but I couldn't make out what he was saying. Sallie's face was peaceful and her rough breathing gradually eased. Callum continued his healing until Mrs Molloy's footsteps could be heard on the wooden landing right outside the door. I'd just started forward, intending to delay her somehow, when Callum came out of his trance and looked up, blinking slowly. He took a deep breath, removing his hand from Sallie's forehead as her mother entered.

Mrs Molloy was carrying a tray with two china cups, and an enamelled mug. The welcome smell of coffee wafted in with her. She looked a little surprised to see the curtains wide open, but after a glance at Sallie, made no comment. Callum took the mug first and glanced at its contents.

'Now, Sallie, this is ma special medicine, an' I only gi' it tae special people,' he told her.

Sallie was already looking brighter, and was well enough to pull a face at the thought of medicine. Callum wasn't put off by her reaction.

'Ah'm goin' tae drink a wee bit first, just tae show ye it's no' so bad. Ah wouldna' ask youse tae drink anything ah wouldna' drink mysel'.' With that, he sipped a little from the white mug, and then offered it to her.

Sallie sipped cautiously at first, her eyes widening as she tasted it. After a few moments, she drank more decisively, and the mug was empty before Callum and I had finished our coffee.

'That's the guid wee girl,' Callum said, returning the enamelled mug to Mrs Molloy. He finished his coffee and stood up, moving more slowly than usual. 'We'll let you make her comfortable,' he said to Mrs Molloy. 'Take your time.'

Mrs Molloy thanked Callum, and we made our way downstairs.

Callum opened the kitchen door and sat on the step, basking in the sunshine. I leaned against the doorframe behind him.

'What's the herbal brew?' I asked.

'A diversion,' he answered, a low chuckle in his voice. 'Many a time, it's wiser no' tae let folks ken what Ah'm doin'. If Ah gie them a drink, an' they get better, they think the secret's in the drink. If Ah just touch them an' they get better, they think the secret's in ma touch. Ah'd rather they thought the secret's in the drink, no' in me. Ah have a couple o' brews; mixes o' herbs that are guid for different complaints. Colds, a bad stomach, women's complaints; that kind o' thing.'

I smiled too, admiring Callum's ingenuity.

After that we were silent for a while. Callum was resting, and I began to realize that he had to use up his own strength when he used his power. There was no sign of Joey, Mrs Molloy's son, but the cows were no longer in the field, so I guessed he was milking them. I looked around the buildings again, seeing the disrepair, the clumsy attempts at fixing things. If the garden wasn't dug and planted soon, there would be no vegetables for the family in the following months. I doubted if there was enough money to buy all the supplies they would need. And whatever cattle Mrs Molloy owned would need rounding up and branding soon, otherwise the calves would be too tempting a target for thieves and unscrupulous ranchers.

'This is a lovely place here,' I remarked. 'This valley, and the views from this house. I sure wouldn't mind staying here a little longer.'

Callum tilted his head back to look up at me. 'Ah was kind o' thinking the same way mysel'. We've had a few fun days o' travelling, but ah could settle to some work now.'

'I haven't ridden a shovel since I left my parents' home, but I guess I can remember how to dig a garden. And I'm a fair hand at mending a fence.'

Callum nodded. 'Aye. I guess Anne Molloy got hersel' a couple o' new hands tae work this place.' He smiled at me. 'Ye got a guid heart, laddie, an' a lot o' strength in ye. Sometime soon ye'll learn how tae use that strength an' your heart together. It's in youse; Ah can see it.'

I was half alarmed, half excited by his words, unsure if I really understood him. Was Callum suggesting that I had a power like his? No doubt I looked as confused and as doubtful as I felt, for Callum laughed and slapped me playfully on the leg.

'There's nae need tae fash yoursel', laddie. You'll no' be needin' much more than your muscles tae be setting this place tae rights.'

It was four days before Callum and I got to see any of Mrs Molloy's Diamond M range. It was a farm, more than a ranch, running a small herd of cattle that were rounded up and sold in conjunction with other small operations. Mrs Molloy regularly sold butter, cheese and eggs to the stores in town, and had sold hay and oats to neighbouring ranches that didn't have farmland. It was a nice place, but after four days of sawing, hammering and digging, it was a relief to get on our horses and ride out to look over some beef.

'This is guid country,' Callum remarked, as we topped a rise in the ground. The main valley that belonged to the ranch was well watered by Beaver Creek and good land for raising crops. To our right was Miller Mesa, the summer ground where the cows would be moved after the spring roundup. 'If she could get enough help, this would be a fine wee place.'

I couldn't help smiling at the way Callum referred to Mrs Molloy. He felt no need to mention her name; she was the first and only woman to him already.

'I'm plumb glad we offered to stay and help,' I said. 'She looked like a weight had been lifted from her shoulders.'

'Aye,' Callum said thoughtfully. 'That puir woman's been carryin' a load all by hersel' since her man died. She couldna' believe we were goin' tae stay, even after she said she couldna' pay verra much.'

'We'll have to parley with the neighbouring ranches about sharing work in the spring roundup,' I said, looking over to the peak of South Baldy to our left. 'Joey was telling me the Rafter K

66

on our west line is the biggest spread around here.'

Callum didn't answer immediately and when I turned to look at him, he was staring intently along the valley. He was bareheaded, as usual, and had to use one hand to keep his shaggy, wind-blown hair out of his eyes.

'D'ye see that?' he asked, pointing ahead. 'Ah reckon that's smoke.'

I followed his gaze and saw a thin line of smoke rising from beyond a low rise in the ground, maybe a quarter of a mile ahead. 'A small camp fire?' I suggested.

'It's on our land,' Callum said disapprovingly. 'Ah reckon we'll take a look, but canny, mind, an' quiet.' He pushed his bay mustang into a jog.

I followed him to where the ground started to rise, forming a brim around the dip from where the smoke came. By now, we could both hear cattle bellowing; mother cows calling to their youngsters, who bawled back. Callum dismounted and drew his Colt Thunderer from his worn black gunbelt.

'Better bring your rifle,' he said quietly, checking the loads in his revolver. I thought of the rustlers that Abe and I had ridden into, and fear gripped me. For a moment I couldn't move, could hardly breathe. Like Callum, I wore my revolver out on the range, and also had my old Winchester 73 on my saddle. I stared at Callum, small and unafraid as he looked to the top of the slope. Scared as I was, I couldn't let him go into danger alone; I couldn't let him down, as I did Abe. Taking a deep breath, I slid from my saddle, and drew the rifle from its boot.

'Guid lad,' Callum said softly, his eyes warm with approval.

CHAPTER SIX

Just those words, and his look, were enough to put heart into me. I followed as he led up the slope, crawling the last few feet so we would not be seen against the sky. I took my hat off, and inched forward through the fresh, spring grass, aiming for a spot between two tussocks of longer grass, so the outline of my head would be less obvious. A few feet to my side, Callum was doing the same. Together, we looked down into the dip in the rolling ground.

A light breeze was blowing in our faces, and brought the smell of burning hide and hair, just like the day Abe died. I swallowed hard, and concentrated on the activity below. Fifteen or so longhorn-cross cattle were gathered to one side of the hollow beneath us, held together by two men on horses. Another man had roped a calf and was dragging it to the fire, where two more men waited for it. The calf's mother bellowed and tried to follow, but was turned back by a swift-riding man on an agile cow pony. The calf was quickly stretched out, branded, ear-marked and released back to the safety of its mother.

I was close enough to see that the grown cows carried the Diamond M brand, Mrs Molloy's brand. The brander was working with a running iron, swiftly drawing a circle and then a letter inside it. Callum let out a low hiss of anger.

'Those are her cows, an' no one's gonna take them frae her while Ah breathe,' he muttered, fury burning in his dark eyes.

Power seemed to be building in him; a violent power ready to explode any time.

'Be careful!' I whispered urgently, seeing him start to rise.

Callum glanced at me, shocking me with the intensity of his gaze. 'There's more o' them than us; the only way is tae be bold. Now cover me, laddie.'

I hastily levered a round into the chamber of my rifle as Callum slipped over the crest of the slope, and started down the other side.

He was almost halfway down before one of the busy men looked up and noticed him. Callum reacted as soon as he knew he'd been spotted. He halted and lined his Colt at the nearest rustler before any of them could react.

'Drop yer guns!' Callum ordered. 'Ma friends're coverin' ye wi' rifles.'

I moved further forward, letting the men below see my head, and the barrel of my rifle.

The rustlers all stopped working, staring at Callum. They kept very still, but none of them moved to surrender immediately. A tall man with a drooping moustache, who had been branding the calves, spoke first.

'Who are you?' he called. 'What authority do you have?'

'Ma name's Callum McGeachin, an' Ah work fer Mrs Molloy. This is her land, an' those are her cows.' Anger throbbed in Callum's voice, exaggerating the rolling burr of his accent. 'Now drop yer guns!'

The rustlers were glancing at one another uneasily. One of the older ones reached slowly to the buckle of his gunbelt and started to unfasten it. Callum's aim remained unwavering on the tall, moustached man, who seemed to be the leader. Slowly, the tall man too began unfastening his gunbelt. The older man tossed his gun and belt to one side, away from himself and his companions, but to one side of Callum too. I began to move closer, careful to keep my rifle up and aimed at the three rustlers standing near the fire. None of us were paying any attention to the cows.

A brown and white cow suddenly burst free of

the bunch, her spotted calf by her side. The nearer
of the two mounted cow ponies immediately spun
on its hocks and sprinted after it, taking its rider by
surprise. The sudden burst of movement startled
everyone, including Callum, who turned slightly to
see what was happening. The leader of the outlaws
acted instantly, snatching his gun from its holster.

'Callum!' I screamed his name as I fired a wild
shot.

Callum flung himself to the left, firing his
Thunderer as he fell. I fired at the scattering
rustlers, working the lever of my rifle frantically.
One of the men staggered as he ran, dropping his
revolver. I never knew whether one of my shots hit
him, or whether it had been Callum's. The injured
man kept going, making for the horses tethered
on the other side of the hollow. The two mounted
men were shooting now, using the rifles booted on
their saddles. I heard lead crack past my ear but I
was more frightened for Callum than for myself.

Callum had found a shallow depression in the
ground and was lying in that, partially covered by
grass and weeds. A bullet smashed the stem of a
cow parsley plant just above his head, decapitating
the flower. Callum was firing back, hampered by
his awkward position. Bullets cracked rapidly from
his double-action revolver. The tall rustler fell, hit
in the leg. He pulled himself to hands and knees
and started crawling away. I was trying to line my

sights on the third dismounted rustler, when a bullet tore across my left shoulder.

I jerked back, almost dropping my rifle. As I gasped for breath, I realized that the cattle below were stampeding. Spooked by the rifle fire, the bunch was headed across the hollow and away, regardless of what might lie in front of them. The two mounted men whirled their horses, spurring them to safety away from the running mob of cattle. Reddish dust swirled in the air as the cattle charged straight over the campfire, scattering the sticks, branding irons and ashes. The third man on foot fled, catching up with the first one we'd shot. He grabbed his injured friend and hauled him towards their anxious, snorting horses.

Their leader, the man Callum had leg-shot, was helpless in the path of the stampede. Callum scrambled to his feet, looking towards the struggling man, then moved back, away from the herd's path. The rustler screamed, a sound of naked terror that rose above the pounding hoofs. The scream ended abruptly as he went down under those hoofs. The cows and calves jostled together in a mindless mass as they passed, leaving the hollow for the open range.

The other rustlers fled, taking the injured man and their leader's horse with them. I leaned forward, feeling sick and shivery, and closed my eyes. I swallowed hard, tasting vomit. A gentle touch on my right shoulder startled me. Callum was there, crouching beside me, looking at me with concern.

'Be easy now, laddie,' he said gently. ' 'Tis all over an' ye did yer part well.'

I gazed down the slope to the battered remains trampled into the ground. 'He died screaming for help,' I said, feeling sick at the thought.

'Aye; it's no' a guid way tae die,' Callum remarked dourly, moving round so he could see the injury on my other shoulder. 'But kinda fittin', tae be killed by the cattle he was tryin' tae steal.'

My shoulder was bleeding where a bullet had torn through the top of it; painful and messy, but not dangerous. I sat on the new spring grass as Callum healed the wound. When he took his hand away, only a faint scar showed on my skin. The pain had gone, and my arm moved easily. Callum washed the dried blood away with water from his canteen, and watched as I fastened my shirt and jacket.

'Ah'd rather no' tell her about this,' he said, glancing at the trampled ground below us. 'But Ah doan' know how we're goin' tae explain the blood and bullet holes on your clothes, Don.'

I thought about that for a moment. 'I surely can't figure out how we can explain blood and bullet marks on my clothes, but only a healed scar on me.'

Callum's eyes widened. 'Ah hadna thought o' that. Still, we need ye tae be fit tae work and tae fight if we find any more o' them bastards makin' off wi' our cattle.'

In the end, when we returned to the ranch, Callum took the horses into the stable, while I dashed in through the door at the back of the house that led directly to our room. I washed and changed into clean clothes before descending to the kitchen, ready for supper.

At supper, we discussed the need for a roundup.

'I don't know where we could get enough men,' Mrs Molloy said, stirring the tea she drank in preference to coffee. 'Or that I could afford to pay them.'

'I could help,' said Joey eagerly. 'I'm nine now and I can ride a horse and throw a rope real well.'

'So can Mamma,' added Sallie, who had completely recovered from her illness. She was looking pleased with herself because she had beaten her brother to the coveted place at the table next to Callum.

'It's gonna take more than four people to round up your cows,' Callum said.

'Don't you usually share the work with the neighbouring outfits?' I asked.

Mrs Molloy frowned slightly. 'We did,' she said. 'We traded some work with the DH Connected, but we mostly used to work with the G over V on big jobs like round up and driving the cows to the railroads. The Rafter K bought out the G over V last fall.'

'Who owns the Rafter K?' Callum asked, helping himself to some more of Mrs Molloy's excellent mashed potato.

'There's three of them,' piped up Joey.

His mother frowned at him. 'Don't interrupt grown-ups when they're talking.' She turned to Callum. 'It's owned jointly by three brothers named Kershaw. The eldest one, Snowy, is married; the other two are bachelors. The Rafter K is by far the biggest spread around here, especially with the G over V land added.'

Callum looked at me. 'Ah reckon we'll ride over tae see them tomorrow, an' have a wee chat about doin' the roundup together.'

I nodded agreement, unable to speak through a mouthful of fried salt pork and delicious gravy.

Good though the main course was, we had to leave room for the dried-apple pie that followed. Callum poured cream over his portion and took his first mouthful, an expression of bliss spreading across his face.

'Ah, Mrs Molloy, you're sure a miracle worker in the kitchen,' he said warmly.

She smiled, her lovely face lighting up with the praise. 'Thank you, Callum. At least I can feed you both properly, even if I can't pay you a proper wage.'

'It wouldna' be right tae leave ye here tae struggle on yer own,' Callum answered.

Mrs Molloy started to say something, then stopped, her gaze intent on Callum's face. She coloured a little, and looked down, fiddling with her spoon. I saw Joey look from one to the other and frown, trying to guess what the grown-ups were thinking.

'I'm glad you decided to stay,' Mrs Molloy said softly, looking first at Callum, and then at me. 'And please, both of you, I'd be honoured if you'd call me Anne.'

'The honour is ours,' Callum said contentedly.

CHAPTER SEVEN

Callum and I rode out to the Rafter K the next morning. Anne Molloy had suggested she come with us, but Callum had talked her out of it.

'Ah doan' like the idea of her riding out when those rustlers could be hereabouts still,' he admitted to me as we let our horses jog across a grassy meadow spangled with spring flowers. 'An' Ah want tae see these Kershaw folk an' get an idea of what they're like, without havin' tae mind what I say in front o' Anne.' He smiled to himself after speaking her name, and a few moments later started to sing a joyful love song. I can't recall the words now, but the details don't matter. Callum sang passionately, with no audience but myself and the mountains; he sang for no other reason than sheer joy.

It was almost noon when we arrived at the Rafter K. We were greeted by the eldest of the Kershaw brothers, Snowy, nicknamed for his very pale fair hair. Without wasting words, he invited us to eat with the family, and we accepted. Everything about the Rafter K was on a larger scale than I'd seen elsewhere. There were two bunkhouses, big enough to take twenty men each, and an adjoining cookhouse. The horses in the corrals were good stock, most likely cross-bred Morgans. Two redbone hounds lay on the porch of the ranch house, a solid, rambling building with windows in unexpected places.

We ate dinner in the kitchen, squeezed in around a long, well-scrubbed pine table. Snowy Kershaw named the other adults present with the minimum of words. His wife, Lily, sat at the far end of the table with their three children. She seemed to spend more time helping her youngest cut up his food, and supervising the girl helper, than she did eating. Mike Kershaw was sitting opposite me. He was the middle one of the three brothers and about thirty, I guessed, though his brown hair had already receded some. Charlie also had brown hair and was the best looking of the three brothers, in spite of a narrow white scar on his forehead. Charlie was sitting next to me, and banged his elbow into me a few times as he rapidly cut up and ate his dinner. Callum had introduced us, and told the Kershaws who we worked for, but business had to wait until the meal was over.

Callum and I showed Mrs Kershaw our appreciation of her food by leaving our plates empty, and took coffee through to the parlour, with the three brothers. Like the ranch itself, this room showed evidence of the brothers' prosperity. There was a large carpet in the centre of the floor, and on it stood a suite upholstered in dark red velvet. Snowy gestured for us to sit down; we all found places except for Charlie, who roamed aimlessly around the room, fiddling with the fringes on the curtains and the antimacassars.

'Ah've come tae talk tae youse about the spring roundup,' Callum explained, addressing himself principally to Snowy.

It was Mike who spoke up. 'Are you running things for Anne Molloy now?'

Callum's brows drew together and I guessed that he disapproved of Mike's use of her first name. 'Aye, Ah'm acting wi' her full authority,' he said, keeping his voice calm. Mike stared at him. 'You can't have been working for her very long.'

'Long enough.'

There was a short silence after Callum's flattening statement. Mike glowered at him, Charlie fidgeted, and Snowy stared at nothing. Callum started again, getting back to what we had come over for.

'Ah expect ye know that the Diamond M used tae join wi' the G over V for the roundup,' Callum said. 'As youse bought the place, Ah was hopin' we could join wi' youse tae do the roundup this year?'

Mike looked at Snowy, who shook his head.

'By the time we've done our own range, we'll need all our hands to move the cattle to their summer ranges,' Mike said, making an apologetic gesture.

'And the just two of you helping out surely won't get it done no faster,' Charlie added scornfully.

I was disappointed by their refusal, and Charlie's remark rankled, but I held on to my temper. Mike spoke again, smiling falsely.

'I'm sorry we can't help, but like Charlie says, it wouldn't be a fair exchange of labour. Anne Molloy's made a brave go of running that place since her husband died, but I don't reckon she can keep it going much longer.' Mike paused for a moment, glancing at me. 'To be honest, I don't reckon there's much future for you in staying with her. We could find work for both of you here, and on better wages.'

'Ah'm happy working for Mrs Molloy,' Callum answered firmly. 'Ah doan need no other job.' His eyes blazed with the intensity of his feelings.

'The same goes for me.' I spoke up clearly.

Mike tried again. 'You surely know that you can't run a ranch, even a bitty one like that, with only two men. We pay thirty dollars a month for top hands like you two.'

It was good money, almost double what Mrs Molloy was paying us, and more than I'd got at the Bar S. I never even thought about accepting the offer though.

'We promised Mrs Molloy we'd do our best for her, and I intend to keep my word,' I said. Callum nodded, the movement taut with anger. 'Ah told ye; Ah work for Mrs Molloy.'

Mike Kershaw didn't like being refused; his mouth set tight with anger. He glanced at Snowy, who shook his head. Making the effort to keep his tone friendly, Mike said:

'Well, the offer remains open, if you change your mind, either of you.'

He looked longer at me, managing a smile. I guessed that he felt I was weaker willed than Callum, and I resented the idea. That resentment seemed to make me more keenly aware of the brothers and what they were thinking.

'Have ye had any problem wi' rustlers?' Callum asked Charlie.

It was Mike who answered. 'Some of our hands chased off a bunch last week,' he said, leaning forward in his chair to get Callum's attention. I carried on watching Charlie; his expression puzzled me. 'They couldn't get close enough to bring any of the varmints down,' Mike went on. 'But we've got enough hands covering our range; it's sure hard for rustlers to work here. Have they been after your stock?'

'Aye,' Callum answered dourly. 'We wounded one o' the bastards an' another got trampled by the cows he was tryin' tae steal. We left his body for the vultures tae eat,' he added, with black satisfaction.

Mike was momentarily disconcerted, his eyes widening as he looked at Callum. Snowy was looking at Callum too, the thoughts in his pale eyes unfathomable – but with Charlie, I somehow got the feeling of glee turning to hate. His face didn't change much, but I was certain of it.

Callum stood up. 'Ah thank youse for yer hospitality. Ah'm just sorry we couldna' work together on the roundup.'

I got up too, as Mike was speaking.

'Don't forget that offer of work here,' Mike said. 'If Anne Molloy can't keep her place going, you may change your minds.'

Callum just nodded by way of answer, and we left.

We rode away quietly from the Rafter K and its guarded, faintly hostile atmosphere. Neither of us wanted to speak until we were well away from the three Kershaw brothers. After half an hour or so, Callum let out a long sigh.

'Well, Don, what did ye make o' that then?' he asked me.

'I reckon Mike Kershaw was lying about the

rustlers hitting them,' I said. 'Charlie was pleased, gleeful, when Mike said that, as if enjoying a joke. And then he got mad when the joke went sour, when you said we killed one and chased them off.'

Callum gave me a penetrating look with his dark eyes. 'Ye could be right,' he mused after a few moments. 'But why would he lie about rustlers stealin' their cattle?'

'Maybe he wants us to think there's too many rustlers for us to keep a handle on, so we're more like to quit working for Mrs Molloy, and join them,' I suggested.

Callum nodded, thinking it through. 'Ah reckon there's some funny business goin' on at the Rafter K. An' Ah doan like that Mike, neether.'

'I guess that's one consolation from them refusing to help with the roundup,' I said brightly. 'At least you won't be working with Mike Kershaw, or any of them.'

Callum chuckled drily. 'Aye. Just so long as we find someone we can work with.'

At Anne Molloy's suggestion, we tried another small ranch outfit, the DH Connected. Dan Hitchins was willing to help out, so we joined his small crew and together swept the range that the two ranches covered. They were long days, combing the valleys and lower mountainsides for cows. We changed horses several times a day, letting them rest between times, but there was no rest for two-legged folk.

The hard work of cowpunching is a young man's job. Callum was the oldest hand riding out on the gather, but he worked tirelessly. He would ride back to the gathering ground, driving half a dozen cows, his face scratched and dead twigs caught in his shaggy hair, for he rarely wore his hat. Anne Molloy and her children had come along to help out too. Anne kept the tally books, marking down each calf branded and keeping a count of how many head we'd found. Joey was helping wrangle the horses, and strutted around as proud as a pup with two tails. Little Sallie mostly stayed at the DH Connected ranch house, playing with the younger Hitchin children. And always, Anne Molloy was the first to see Callum when he returned to the gathering ground. She looked up at the sound of any rider approaching. If it was not the man she was waiting for, she turned back quickly to her work. If it was Callum, her eyes warmed and she would be smiling when he saw her. Having found one another again, they were content and went about their business.

The end of spring roundup was a great relief to all the ranches. To celebrate, a dance was to be held in the largest saloon in Ridgeway. Ranch families came in from all over to enjoy the fun, children packed into wagons and go-to-town dresses packed into gunny sacks. We all helped to get the saloon ready, moving tables and chairs to make a big space for dancing. The bottles of hard liquor were hidden away, but beer and hard cider were available, along with fresh lemonade, sarsaparilla and root beer. Four musicians gathered by the saloon piano to discuss what to play, and to tune up together. Besides the piano, there was a fiddle, mandolin, guitar, and a penny whistle. I saw Callum in conversation with the musicians, singing them a snatch of something I couldn't make out over the general noise.

By the time the dance was due to start, I was as excited as the children. We split up to change our clothes in various townhouses, as everyone, young and old, wanted to be dressed in their best for the occasion. The saloon was lively when I returned, mostly with men taking in a couple of beers before the dancing started. I spotted Callum at the long bar and pushed my way through to join him there.

'Have ye seen Anne yet?' he asked, tilting his head back to look up at me.

Callum had changed from his usual blue Levis into a pair of smart black trousers, and wore a soft-collared white shirt. He had gotten Anne Molloy to trim his wild black hair a little, though it was still long enough to brush his shirt collar.

'No,' I answered, taking a beer. 'But I did see the Kershaws.'

Callum shrugged a little. 'Ah weel, they'se got a right tae come an' dance too.' He looked away from me and around the room. His expression changed in a moment, his eyes lighting up and a smile starting: I knew he had seen Anne Molloy.

She stood just inside the saloon doors, her children on either side. Her fine dress was royal blue, lightened with creamy lace that cascaded from the neckline and the bell-shaped sleeves. Standing there, in the elaborate draperies of her bustled dress, and with her dark hair plaited into a crown around her head, Anne Molloy was as lovely as a Greek statue, but warm and alive. Her blue eyes sparkled as she saw Callum and me approaching. Callum took her hand and gazed at her with open adoration.

'Ah must ha' the first dance wi' ye, or Ah'll no' dance at all,' he told her.

'It would be my pleasure,' Anne replied, colouring a little as she returned his gaze.

They looked a strange pair, Anne so elegant and Callum wild-haired and roguish.

The caller announced the first dance and they moved away to find a set. I looked down at little Sallie, who was wearing a pretty dress of dark green plaid. She was gazing about at the crowd with wide eyes, so like her mother's.

'Would you honour me with a dance?' I asked, holding out my hand.

Sallie smiled suddenly and put her hand into mine, following me on to the dance floor.

There were far more men than women, of course, and other young girls were dancing, all treated carefully by the older dancers. A 'floor manager' had been appointed for the evening, to see that all the men had a turn at dancing with the women. After the first exhilarating dance, Callum reluctantly surrendered Anne Molloy first to me, then to a succession of other men. I thought he might sit out other dances, but the pull of the music was too strong and he took turns with the other women – and soon proved himself a popular partner, for he danced as well as he did most other things. I danced as often as I could find a partner, and enjoyed myself more than I had in many weeks.

For two hours, the saloon echoed to the pounding of boots on its wooden floor and the swishing of long skirts. It was nearly suppertime when Callum joined the band on the small stage. I thought he was going to call the next dance in the usual way, but to everyone's surprise, he sang to the music instead.

'First couple separate, go up an' round the ring. Ye pass yer partner comin' out; ye pass them comin' in.' Callum sang at the top of his powerful voice, somehow making himself heard over the band. As he sang the chorus, his eyes were on

Anne Molloy, dancing with Mike Kershaw.

There was tremendous applause for Callum when the dance finished. He grinned, bowed once, and jumped down off the stage. The regular caller announced that the next dance was to be a waltz, followed by a break for supper. As I turned to look for a partner, I saw Anne Molloy and Mike Kershaw together on the dance floor. He had hold of her arm, and she was shaking her head. Callum was pushing his way through the crowd towards them, his eyes sparking with anger.

CHAPTER EIGHT

Forgetting about finding a partner for myself, I began hurrying to where Callum was about to confront Mike Kershaw. Anne Molloy was trying to detach her arm from Kershaw's grip.

'I'm sorry,' she was saying. 'I've already promised this dance to someone else.'

'You can dance with him later,' Mike Kershaw answered, trying to catch hold of her other arm. 'If you still want to after you've danced with me.'

'The lady disnae wish tae dance wi' ye,' Callum snapped, arriving at Anne's side. He glared up at the taller, younger man.

Kershaw ignored him; he was a little unsteady on his feet and spoke slightly too loudly, as drunks do. 'You surely aren't turning me down to dance with your hired help?' he asked Anne Molloy, leaning towards her.

'I'll dance with whoever I wish,' she answered

spiritedly. 'Please let go of me!' She tugged her arm away, causing Mike Kershaw to sway.

He caught his balance, cursing vigorously.

'Mind yer gab around the ladies,' Callum said sharply. 'Now leave the lady alone afore there's trouble.'

The raised voices had started to attract attention. I saw Charlie Kershaw's face among those watching the confrontation. Mike now turned on Callum.

'I don't take orders from you, you runt. No wonder she took you on, she couldn't afford to pay a full-grown man,' Mike sneered.

I couldn't believe what he was saying, or that he was foolish enough to do so. Anne's face flushed with anger, and her blue eyes took on a steely tint. Callum's whole body was taut with imminent fury as he took Anne's arm to lead her away. I watched with a kind of numb horror, waiting for the explosion I knew would surely come. Mike Kershaw's face contorted with jealousy and anger.

'How does she pay you, McGeachin?' he called. 'Or is that pretty widow's *bed* and board enough?'

He barely had time to finish the sentence before Callum spun and lunged at him.

Callum went for Mike Kershaw with both fists, battering him backwards as the crowd scattered. Mike twisted and flailed about, trying to fend off the relentless blows. He tried to grab Callum's shirt, but Callum neatly stepped back out of reach. I saw Charlie Kershaw run to help his brother, and before I knew what I was doing, I was moving too. I reached Charlie before he got to Callum, and grabbed his shoulder. Charlie turned round, roaring, and swung at me. I jumped aside and aimed a punch at his face. My fist glanced off his cheek, but I had diverted him from Callum.

Charlie caught me a heavy blow on my shoulder, but I stood my ground. I'd never been much of a fighter but I wanted to keep him away from Callum. I did my best to keep dodging, fending off Charlie's punches and swinging at him myself when I had the chance. He landed some hard blows on my ribs and one on my face, just on my cheekbone. The fight probably didn't last much more than a minute, but it felt longer to me. Now and again, as we dodged about, I caught glimpses of Callum fighting Mike. Then others moved in to break up the fights.

I was happy to stop as soon as someone grabbed Charlie. Callum was yelling furiously, struggling in the grip of two larger men.

'Youse all heard wha' he said about her!' he shouted. 'Ah'll no' stand by an' let any man speak like that tae a guid woman like Anne Molloy.'

Mike Kershaw was a few feet away from him, wiping blood from his face with the back of his hand. His thinning hair was dishevelled and he was breathing heavily as he glared at Callum.

'Damn you, McGeachin,' he spat. 'Damn you and Anne Molloy, both.'

Callum stopped struggling and took a slow, deep breath. I saw his expression change as he started to concentrate. He was summoning his power, but I didn't know for what purpose. The men holding him thought he had calmed down, and relaxed slightly. Callum's eyes regained their full focus, aimed with fierce intent on Mike Kershaw. I was expecting something to happen, but Callum moved so fast I could barely follow. He burst free of the men holding him and had reached Mike Kershaw before anyone knew what was happening. Callum seized the front of Kershaw's shirt and hauled the taller man around, throwing him to the floor. Kershaw landed hard on the wooden boards, sliding to a stop right in front of Anne Molloy.

Callum bounded after him and landed with both knees on Mike Kershaw's back. Grabbing a handful of Kershaw's hair, Callum ruthlessly pulled his head up.

'Now, apologize tae the lady,' he ordered.

Kershaw grunted and heaved, trying to throw Callum off his back. Callum barely budged; he slammed Kershaw's face into the lumber floor and then hauled it up again.

'Ye slandered this guid woman in front o' all these people. Now yer goin' tae apologise tae her afore them.'

There was a murmur of approval in the room. Those who hadn't heard the talk that started the fight, had had it repeated to them since.

'I'm sorry for what I said.' Mike Kershaw forced the words out. Blood dripped from his nose.

'Louder,' Callum insisted. His muscles were bunched, ready to strike again.

Resentment burned in Kershaw's eyes, but he had no choice but to obey.

'I'm sorry for what I said,' he repeated as clearly as he could with Callum kneeling on his back.

Callum released his grip on Kershaw's hair, and got quickly to his feet. He watched as Charlie and Snowy Kershaw helped their brother up. I saw murder in Mike's eyes, and felt it in him, as clear as anything, but he let himself be taken away and out of the saloon. Anything the brothers said was drowned out in the excited conversation that rose. I thought about going after them, to see what they were doing. However, if they saw me, they might turn on me, as Callum's friend, and I knew I couldn't fight them. I chose the safer option of letting them go.

Callum ran his hands through his hair, pushing it back off his face and then smoothing it down again. His fierce power seemed to change in him, the hard-edged fury turning to bright charisma as he smiled, his attention on Anne Molloy. In a moment, he gathered her into his arms, holding her for a waltz.

'Ah believe this was ma dance?' he asked, grinning impishly. 'Start playin',' he called to the band.

Anne gazed at him in wonder as they began to dance. A cowhand gave a whoop and seized hold of his girl to start dancing too. The music rose as the band gained more confidence. The fight was put into the background as more and more people chose to enjoy the moment and the dancing. Callum danced with Anne for the rest of the night.

It was almost dawn when we returned to the Diamond M. I rode Luke, half-asleep and trusting my horse to find his own way in the starlight. The children slept in the back of the jolting wagon, bundled in blankets and cradled by sacks of groceries. Callum drove the wagon, Anne beside him on the seat. I could see their shapes, black against the black night, Anne leaning against Callum's shoulder. Now and again I caught the murmur of their voices but what they said was a secret between themselves, and the brilliant stars above.

It was hard to get up the next morning, especially as Callum looked remarkably bright and fresh. He and I shared the hired men's room at the back of the house. While I was barely awake, he was already up and dressed. I sat up slowly, groaning and cautiously feeling the tender spots on my face where Charlie Kershaw's fists had left their mark.

'Guid morning,' Callum greeted me, tugging a comb through his hair. 'Ah never did thank ye last night, fer comin' tae help wi' Charlie.'

'Are you going to thank me now?' I asked, reaching for my plaid shirt.

'Ah can do better than that.' Callum stuck the comb in the pocket of his Levis and came to sit on the edge of my rumpled bed. I sat still and let him place his fingertips gently against my face. The warmth of his touch was remarkable, and soothing. In a few moments he had healed away my bruises and pain.

'Is that enough thanks for ye?' he asked, standing again.

I nodded, then spoke. 'Callum, when are you going to tell Anne about your power?'

Callum's expression became serious. 'Ah doan know,' he said slowly.

'You'll have to. Sooner or later, she'll find out; something will happen. . . .'

Callum was studying the plain gold ring he wore on the little finger of his left hand. 'The power has run strong in ma family for generations. I guess there wouldna' be those generations if they hadna' found women willin' tae marry them. It's no' easy though.' He paused, and I guessed he was thinking of something, or someone, from his past.

I started to pull on my shirt. 'Anne Molloy is a

rare kind of woman, but still a woman for all that. I know that women like surprises, but they don't like shocks.'

Callum grinned suddenly. 'Ah'll bear yer advice in mind. An' Ah'll see ye downstairs for breakfast.' He was out the door and away in a sudden burst of energy.

I shook my head and finished getting dressed.

The day's work was enlivened by Callum's singing, and by Joey's exuberance. The boy delighted in the company of men, after so long with only his mother and little sister for company, and it was impossible not to respond. I'd given him his first taste of beer at the dance, and now he strutted around, convinced he was almost full grown. He helped us digging out an irrigation ditch, and pestered Callum to teach him some more about roping.

Both children were plumb tuckered out by suppertime, and went quietly to bed. I sat in the parlour a little longer, glad to sit and rest a while. Anne sat before the piano, and lifted the lid. She stroked the keys carefully, listening to the sounds.

'It's difficult to keep it in tune,' she said, mostly to Callum, who was standing behind her. 'I used to love playing it, but there never seemed to be enough time, after Tom died.' She pressed a few soft chords.

Callum hummed the notes after her.

'Tom thought it was an extravagance, really, and it was such trouble to haul it all the way out here, but I was glad we did.' Anne started playing something from memory, her slender fingers light across the keyboard.

Callum was close to her, one hand resting on her shoulder as she played. When she finished, they conferred quietly and a song was chosen. Anne played and Callum sang, his voice warm and caressing for all its rough tones. It was a rare pleasure to sit and listen to them, but music did not absorb me so deeply, and I found myself dozing in my chair. Covering a yawn, I got up and wished them good night. I left them together and went straight to my bed.

I slept deeply until early the next morning. I woke, feeling refreshed and comfortable, and rolled over, luxuriating in the softness of a feather mattress. Our room was filled with the grey pre-dawn light. The light was strong enough to show me that Callum's bed was still neat, and had not been slept in. I was half-asleep and pondering on this, when the door opened and Callum slipped in quietly. He was dressed only in his trousers and carried shirt and boots. He glanced at me, and saw I was awake. Then it came to me and I knew whose bed he had spent the night in. I felt an unexpected flash of jealousy.

'Och, dinna frown at me like that, laddie,'

Callum said, half amused, half annoyed. 'Ah'm no' a saint, Ah'm a man o' flesh, like ye. An' a woman has her needs too, same as a man. Me an' Anne know what we're about.'

'I'm sorry,' I said, wondering why I felt so hurt. 'I guess it's none of my business.'

Callum tilted his head to one side as he looked at me. 'One day ye'll find the woman ye can lose yer heart tae, an' ye'll feel the way Ah do now.' He smiled suddenly and moved away to look out of the window. The light was rosy now with the coming dawn, and the snow on the mountain tops was flushed with colour. Callum gazed at the view for a minute, and sighed. 'This is a braw country for sure; Ah could bide here forever. An' now Ah got the best o' all reasons tae stay.'

Those soft words would come back to me later and bring the sting of tears to my eyes.

CHAPTER NINE

The following days were peaceful and filled with sunshine. Anne Molloy and Sallie worked in the truck garden, planting and tending vegetables. Callum, Joey and I harrowed the fields and sowed oats and wheat. We worked on clearing and improving the irrigation ditches in the valley. The ditches were needed to water the grass that would be cut for hay in the winter. In the evenings we talked and planned the future of the Diamond M. When Sallie grew bored of the talk of the cost of hiring haying machines, I would tell her fairy stories. I also started reading *Ivanhoe* out loud to Callum and Anne, or listened to them singing together. At night, I had the hired men's room to myself, for Callum was sharing Anne's bed.

At first I found myself resenting their love, and feeling bad that I did. I admired all I saw about Anne, but I wasn't drawn to her in the way that

Callum was, so I was puzzled by my feelings, and worked hard not to let them show.

One day, we found the ditches dry, and barely a trickle of water in the creek. Callum scowled at the depressing sight.

'What the Hell?' he said in frustration. 'That couldna' just happen overnight.'

I looked back up the winding valley, tracing the course of Beaver Creek as far as I could see. 'A rock slide or something must surely have dammed it.'

'We'd best gang an' find out,' Callum decided.

Joey grinned at us. 'I'd rather be riding than digging ditches anyhow.'

Callum snorted and gave him a gentle cuff on the back of his head, but there was laughter in his eyes.

We saddled our horses and rode back along Beaver Creek. About a mile above the ranch buildings, the valley narrowed where a spur of high ground projected out. The creek ran close to the steeply rising ground at that point. As I'd guessed, a rock slide had broken away from the slope and dammed the water. Raw, reddish rock showed above the pile of debris. A mound of mud, rock and broken trees lay before us.

'Hellfire!' Joey exclaimed. 'Look at all that mess!' He slipped off his horse and ran towards the rock slide.

'Hey! Careful there, ye gowk!' Callum called, hurriedly dismounting too. 'That gurt heap isna safe tae be climbin' on.'

Joey stopped and looked back. 'I want to see what's happened to the water.'

'An' so ye will, but we'll be gang carefu', ye ken?' Callum insisted.

We climbed cautiously to the top of the rock slide to look at the valley beyond. The creek had spread out, spilling beyond its banks. In time it would find its way around the rock slide and make a new path down the valley.

'What are we going to do?' asked Joey. 'We need the water downstream for the stock, and for the fields.'

'We're gonna have tae shift all this we're sitting on now,' Callum answered, studying the side of the valley and the rocks thoughtfully.

'It'll take weeks to clear this away!' Joey wailed. 'Even if we trade work with the DH Connected.'

'We can get it done a wee bit quicker than that,' Callum said. 'Ah reckon a well-placed blast should clear away this muckle pile o' rocks, enough tae let the water come through anyway.'

'Dynamite?' I asked, startled. 'Have you ever used it?'

'Ah worked in a silver mine a wee while an' Ah handled it then. 'Tis safe enough until ye put the detonator caps on.'

'Why did you quit working in the mines?' Joey asked. He turned his head as he spoke, to watch an eagle soaring above us, and missed the flash of pain in Callum's eyes.

'Ah dinna care tae be working underground, in the dark,' Callum answered.

I felt there were memories locked in Callum's mind, memories perhaps of mining accidents and suffering that he didn't want to tell the boy. Callum looked full at me and I knew I was right. There had been those too badly hurt for Callum to save; men who had died under his hands as he struggled to heal them. I started to understand how his gift was also a curse.

'We'd best be getting ourselves back to your ma,' I said briskly to Joey. 'Dinner will be about ready, and she'll not be pleased if we're late.'

Joey grinned. 'I'm so hungry, my middle's all one big hole inside.' He began picking his way back over the broken rocks.

Callum gave me a grateful smile, and we set ourselves to the task of carefully climbing down again.

The next morning, Callum rode into Ridgeway to buy dynamite and the detonator caps. I stayed at the ranch to catch up with some chores I could do by myself. It was close to noon when I saw three riders approaching along the trail to the house. Even at a distance I could see none of them was

Callum. I put down the saddle I had been clean-
ing, and went to the house to warn Anne. She was
in the parlour with her children, listening to them
practising their spelling. Joey stopped in the
middle of a word when I opened the parlour door,
glad of the diversion.

'Go on, Joey,' Anne instructed, darting a glance
at me. 'Necessary?'

Joey took a deep breath, and spelled the word
slowly and correctly.

'Good,' Anne said. 'Now copy it neatly on to
your slate, ten times, please.' When Joey was
settled, she came to the door where I stood.

'Visitors approaching,' I told her. 'Three men.'

Her face lit up for a moment, then became wary.
'Three? The Kershaws?' Dislike coloured Anne's
eyes but the tradition of range hospitality was
strong. She told her delighted children to put
their books away and go play outside.

Anne's guess was right; it was the Kershaw brothers. I stayed a couple of paces behind her as she
walked out to greet them, and invited them to
water their horses and come inside. Snowy handed
his reins to Charlie and moved towards us without
uttering a greeting. Mike dismounted and made a
show of looking around. I was pleased to see the
marks of his fight with Callum still on his face.

'Where's McGeachin?' Mike asked, his tone
barely civil. He let his eyes wander up and down

Anne Molloy's body. She was wearing a simple cotton dress with a faded print of small flowers, and her hair pinned up in a braid. No matter how workaday her clothes, it was impossible to mistake her for anything but a lady.

'Callum is not at the ranch house at the moment,' Anne answered coolly. Her lovely face was as calm and unrevealing as that of a marble statue.

Mike looked at me contemptuously. 'I see he done left his shadow behind.'

'There are worse people than Callum McGeachin to follow,' I answered sharply, before regretting that I had risen to his bait.

Anne led us inside and provided coffee, making tea for herself. The Kershaw brothers settled themselves around the parlour, filling the room with their presence. Charlie, the youngest, was the first to speak.

'I see you got some repairs done about the place at last,' he said, spite underlying his tone.

'Callum and Don have worked hard,' Anne answered, stirring her fragrant tea.

'You got your round-up done all right?' Mike spoke up. 'We're sorry we couldn't spare the help for you.'

'It was fine, thank you. We had a good crop of calves this year.' Anne allowed a touch of satisfaction to show. 'And there should be plenty of feed.'

The room was quiet for a few moments. The sounds of the children's voices drifted in through the open window. I was aware of Snowy's pale eyes on me, while Mike watched Anne. Charlie examined the sheet music on the piano, then suddenly spoke.

'The Diamond M is still a real small operation, though. It's been pretty lean for you since Molloy died, hasn't it?'

'I've managed,' Anne said.

'That's just it,' Mike took up his cue. 'You've just been getting by, managing. You've done your best, I'm sure, but it's no life for a woman. You deserve better than this struggle.' For once there was something like sincerity in his voice. 'I hate to see you managing out here on your own.'

'We want to buy this place off you,' Charlie interrupted. 'We'll give you a fair price and cash on the barrel-head.'

'You can move back east,' Snowy said. It was the first complete sentence he'd spoken since arriving.

'I like it here,' Anne answered. She looked at each of the Kershaw brothers in turn as she spoke. 'This ranch is Joey's inheritance. Tom and I worked hard to build what I have now. The mountain air is good for Sallie. And I love the mountains; I feel closer to God here.'

'Well, you don't need to move far,' Mike said. 'But we can make a real good offer. You could set

Joey up in some business when he's of age. You wouldn't have to feed hogs, or clean chicken coops or worry about getting up hay for the winter.'

'I don't want to sell,' Anne said firmly.

Charlie snorted in exasperation. 'It don't make no sense for you to hang on when we make you a good offer.'

'I don't want to sell the Diamond M,' Anne repeated.

I felt it was time to speak up. 'That seems clear enough to me. Mrs Molloy knows her own mind on the matter.'

Charlie swung round and glared at me. 'You stay out of this. You ain't nothin' but the hired help and not even the one she's. . . .'

A deep fury woke within me and I felt a sudden surge of power. I remembered what Callum had said to me the day we arrived here.

'*Ye got a guid heart, laddie, an' a lot o' strength in ye. Sometime soon ye'll learn how tae use that strength an' your heart together. It's in youse; Ah can see it.*'

That strength suddenly seemed to blossom in me, filling me with confidence. Charlie saw it and his words trailed off.

Into the silence came Joey's voice, carried on the breeze through the open window.

'I bet you Mike Kershaw wouldn't have dared stay if Callum was here. You sure missed something, being asleep when Callum threw Kershaw to the floor and made him apologize to Mother in front of the whole town and everyone.'

'You told me about it already,' Sallie answered impatiently.

'Damn-fool lying kids!' Mike Kershaw spat. His handsome face was darkened with anger and shame.

'Joey's only speaking truth about what happened,' I commented.

Mike stood up, his movements jerky. 'I am not afraid of McGeachin,' he snapped. 'He took me by surprise at the dance. If I ever tangle with that sawn-off son-of-a-bitch again, he'll be the one eating dirt!'

'Mind your language in this house,' Anne snapped, her eyes flashing.

Mike stopped abruptly, aware of his breach of range courtesy.

Charlie took up the attack. 'We aim to have this range, dammit!'

'Mrs Molloy doesn't want to sell,' I answered, almost calmly. I moved slowly towards Mike Kershaw. 'There's no deal here. You'd best leave now.'

I was unarmed, while the Kershaws were all wearing pistols, but I felt more confident than I ever had before. The feeling of power, like Callum's power, coursed through me, as heady as strong spirits. Mike Kershaw saw something in my face he'd never seen there before, and it worried him. He glanced at Snowy, the eldest. Snowy got to his feet and nodded at Anne Molloy.

'Remember our offer,' he said, forcing the few words out with an effort.

With that, he led the way from the parlour.

As Mike passed Anne, he stopped and said. 'You should think more carefully about your choices. I could have made things easier for you.'

Anne looked at him steadily. 'I regret nothing.'

Charlie chuckled nastily. 'She's made her bed, an' McGeachin's lying in it.'

I started towards him but Anne held up a hand. 'He's speaking the truth,' she said, looking straight into Mike Kershaw's eyes.

For a moment, I thought Mike Kershaw was going to hit that fine, brave woman. Instead he made a wordless sound of pain and anger, and stormed from the room. Charlie contented himself with glaring at myself and Anne, then followed his brothers. I went to the door to watch them mount up and ride away, my spine straightened by the confidence I'd discovered in myself. It was then I realized why Callum and Anne's love had been bothering me. Since Abe's death, I'd relied on Callum as a support and friend. Anne had taken some of him away from me and I'd been jealous of his attention to her, not wanting to share. But just now, I'd found that I didn't need to be his shadow, or anyone's shadow, any longer. When the Kershaws were out of sight, I returned to the parlour.

Anne was sitting on a chair, clutching a cushion against herself as though it would protect her. She looked up at me, no longer a marble statue, but a shaken woman.

'Thank you, Don,' she said. 'I'm so glad you were here.' She looked at me more thoughtfully. 'When things got nasty, there was something new about you. You reminded me . . . of Callum.'

I smiled. 'He's a remarkable man; I've sure learnt a lot from him.'

Anne smiled too. 'Yes, remarkable. I never met a man like him; you're the only one who has something of that. . . .' The words stumbled to a halt.

'Power?'

'Yes, power.' Anne thought about it. 'I might almost be afraid of Callum, if I didn't love him so.'

'He'd never hurt you,' I said with certainty.

Anne's blue eyes opened wide. 'No, never. There's no evil in Callum, but if he wanted to, I'm sure he could use his . . . power . . . to destroy.'

I offered the best comfort I could. 'All that Callum is, and has, is at your service.'

A gentle smile warmed Anne's face. 'I know.'

CHAPTER TEN

When Callum got back and heard about the Kershaws' visit, he was mad enough to chew nails and spit rivets.

'Ah wish Ah'd been here!' he exclaimed. 'They'd never have dared trouble ye if Ah was home.'

Anne and I had expected this kind of reaction. We made sure the children were about their evening chores in the yard before giving Callum a carefully edited account of what had been said and done.

'Don stood up to them,' Anne said soothingly. 'He almost frightened me, the way he looked at Charlie and Mike.' She slid her hands around Callum's waist, pulling him close, then rubbed up and down his back.

Callum gradually relaxed, sighing softly into her sleek hair. 'Ah'm sorry, hen. Ah dinna trust those

Kershaws, no' a one of them.'

'No harm was done.' Anne continued her gentle massage.

'Aye.' Callum looked up, straight at me as I sat by the kitchen table. 'Ah'm grateful tae ye, Don.' He held Anne close to him. 'Truly grateful.'

The next morning I learned that Callum had more cause for his worry than I'd imagined. We were riding out to blast the landslide, on our own as Callum had insisted that Joey stay behind, in spite of the boy's pleadings.

'Ah learned somethin' interesting in town yesterday,' Callum told me. 'When Ah was buying the dynamite an' caps, the shopkeeper said it was the second time in a week he'd sold some. Ah asked him who else had been buying, an' he said Snowy Kershaw had bought dynamite just three days back.'

I thought about this. 'Did Snowy say what he wanted it for?'

Callum shook his head. 'Snowy dinna say anythin' he doesna need tae.'

'And not always that much,' I added drily.

Callum grinned briefly. 'Ah dinna think so much of it afore ye told me he'd been here wi' his brothers, trying tae buy Anne out. It seems tae me that those Kershaws might not be above fixing things tae push her decision.'

It took me a few moments to grasp what he meant. 'You mean they'd deal from the bottom of the deck and get Anne to sell by cutting off her water?'

'Could be, laddie, could be,' Callum answered.

When we reached the rock slide, Callum took his time over deciding where to set the dynamite. He studied the debris pile from all angles, trying to find the best way of clearing the creek bed without leaving too much to be moved by hand.

'Ah learnt something about rock in the mine, but Ah'm no expert,' he told me, eyeing the new, unweathered rock of the valley side above the landslide. 'Ye see that fault along there?' He pointed and I tried to see what he meant. 'If Ah get the blast wrong, Ah could bring that down too. There's nae use bringing down more on what we already got.'

'My ma always told me that brains in the head saved blisters on the feet,' I quoted.

Callum moved closer to the point where the landslide had started, scrambling agilely over the outflung debris. He studied the bare face of the rock and as I watched him, I saw his fingers flexing against the boulder he was perched on, as if seeking information from the stone itself. After a few minutes, he made his way back to me.

'Ah'd swear tha' no' a natural landslide,' he said vehemently. 'Ah'm sure that rock's been blasted, but there's nae way tae prove it.'

'If it was the Kershaws, they could have come down Blaine Draw there,' I suggested. 'It leads up to the old G Over V range they own now. If we search, I reckon we might find some sign.'

Callum's face brightened, and he nodded. 'Guid thinking, Don. But we haftae clear this an' get the water flowing first.'

I'd never handled dynamite, so I just watched as Callum carefully set the charges where he thought best. I noticed that he handled the sticks of explosive with more freedom than the cylindrical blasting caps.

'Nasty wee things,' Callum said, showing me one. 'It dinna take much tae get one tae explode, an' they'll take yer fingers off easy. Ah'll have tae store the rest somewhere the bairns cannae find them.'

At last everything was ready, and we watched from what Callum thought would be a safe distance as the charges blew. Rocks and shattered fragments of trees scattered liberally around the valley. A great cloud of dust obscured our view of the landslide for a minute or two. I wrinkled my nose at the foul smell of the dynamite smoke. When everything had cleared up, we could see that Callum had judged things well. The great pile of rocks and trees that had come down originally, had now been broken smaller and scattered over a wider area. We had brought shovels, tied to a pack horse, and with a couple of hours work, cleared away enough of the remaining rubble to let the creek flow again.

'That's a fine sight,' I said contentedly, watching the damned-up water spilling through its new course to fill the dry bed downstream.

Callum knelt and dipped his hands in the fast-running water, splashing it over his face.

'Och, that's cauld!' he exclaimed. 'But guid, real guid.'

We rested a while and ate some of the bread and cheese Anne had packed for us. I found some wild onion plants, and we ate the bulbs raw with our food. Feeling much refreshed, Callum and I mounted our horses and rode slowly up Blaine Draw. It didn't take too long to find evidence that other riders had been this way a couple of days ago. We kept searching, and were soon sure that three or four men had ridden this way, down from the G over V, but had gone no further on to Diamond M land than the area around the rock-slide.

'They wasna passing through,' Callum commented when we halted to confer. 'They came here for some reason, and went back where they come frae. It musta' been the Kershaws, come tae dry up our water.'

I kicked my feet free of my stirrups to stretch my

legs. 'So what do we do? It's going to be harder'n hell to prove it was them, or even that the landslide was caused by a blast.'

Callum let his horse snatch a mouthful of sweet spring grass as he thought. 'Ah want tae gang over their range an' take a look. Ah dinna ken what we'll find, but Ah doan' want tae just sit an' wait for them tae come tae us.'

I wasn't sure what use it would be to ride about over the Kershaw's range, but I was willing to follow Callum. 'What are we going to do with the pack horse?' I asked.

'If we turn him loose, he'll find his ain way home frae here,' Callum said.

'Might give Anne a scare if he comes back without us,' I pointed out. 'I'll write a couple of notes, and fix them to the bridle and harness, so she knows we're fine.'

Callum smiled. 'Guid thinking, Don; Ah'd hate tae ha' worried her like that.'

I did as I suggested, and Callum carefully added his name to mine. When all was ready, I turned the pack horse loose and sent him on his way with a slap on his rump.

Our horses climbed steadily along the wooded sides of the draw. Now and again we saw traces of where others had recently passed the same way. We didn't speak much as we made our way through the dappled sunlight. Callum rode like a hunter, his eyes searching for signs of the enemy. I was wondering what we should do if we did find the Kershaws or their men. We hadn't intended looking for trouble, and though we were both wearing our revolvers, I had left my rifle back at the ranch house.

After an hour or so, we had reached the long, winding valley of the east fork of Dallas Creek, which marked the border between the Diamond M and the easternmost range of the Rafter K. South Baldy rose almost ahead of us, and away to our left, the peaks of the Mount Sneffels range were crowned with snow still.

'Where now?' I asked, gazing at the immense, uninhabited landscape.

Callum pointed across the valley, to a flatter treeless area immediately below South Baldy. 'Ah was thinkin' about why the Kershaws might want so much land. Surely their cows canna be breedin' so fast they need tae buy two mair ranches in less'n a year or so. Ah got to thinkin' about those devils who were branding our calves, and where they was gang tae take those calves. The Kershaws ha' got plenty o' room tae be hiding them.'

Callum's words jogged my memory. 'Remember I thought Mike Kershaw lied when he said they'd had stock taken by rustlers?' I said. 'If we believed him, we'd rule him out as the thief.'

Callum nodded. 'Well, let's ride over that way

117

an' see if we can find any o' their cows. Ah'm interested tae know what kind o' brand they got on them.'

We rode for almost another hour before we found some steers grazing in the upland meadow on the other side of the valley. One or two raised their heads to watch us as we approached. One, a black and white steer with a broken horn, looked familiar to me. I pointed it out to Callum.

'Can you see the brand on that one?'

We circled it at a distance, trying not to scare it into moving off.

'Looks like Circle HS tae me,' Callum said. 'I doan' recall Anne mentioning that brand anywhere around here.'

'Circle HS. No, there isn't one in San Juan county!' I said, the words tumbling out faster and faster. 'That's the brand that those rustlers were changing the Bar S cows to. I remember seeing that steer in their gather. Abe and me pulled it out of a bog hole last summer. The men that brought this beef here must be the ones who killed Abe!'

'An' it's on Rafter K range,' Callum added. 'Nae wonder they didna' want to let us join their round up, when they've got cows wi' all kinds o' brands on their range.'

Both Callum and I had been paying attention to the beef, and to our speculations about the Kershaws, rather than to the range around us. I was some surprised when my horse, Luke, lifted his head and neighed a vigorous greeting to another horse. Callum and I both turned in our saddles, following Luke's gaze. Four riders had appeared from a fold in the ground and were heading towards us at a brisk trot. One man was black, far darker skinned than me, and another was as skinny as a strip of rawhide. I glanced at those two, and stared longer at the others. The nearest was shorter even than Callum and the other one . . . the longer I looked, the more sure I was that he was the man who had killed my brother.

They were some distance away, but I could see a shock of recognition in him. He might have seen Abe's body close-to, and we looked very much like one another.

'He murdered my brother!' I cried, reaching for my revolver.

'Then he willna' want a witness alive,' Callum answered. 'Come on, laddie.'

He started to turn his horse, but I held my ground and fired at Abe's murderer. It was a very long shot for a revolver and I was firing fast, full of anger. The shot did no harm to anyone. The rustlers began drawing rifles from their saddle boots, while urging their horses on faster. I knew it was no use trying to outshoot them, and thrust my revolver away as I spun Luke around to chase after Callum.

We leaned forward in our saddles, letting the horses race on. Rifle fire cracked sporadically from behind us. I knew in my head that it was hard for them to hit us when they were riding fast themselves, but every time I heard a shot, my heart skipped a beat. The skin on my back crawled, anticipating the shot that would knock me from my saddle. More shots split the air and Callum suddenly cried out in pain. A bullet had torn through his thigh muscle, painful, but not immediately dangerous. I called to him and he looked across at me, his face set with determination.

'Ah can keep riding.'

We had no other choice.

Our horses raced back across the wide valley we had recently crossed and gallantly tackled the long wooded slope up to the top of Blaine Draw. The rustlers must have ridden some distance already that day, for they did not gain on us. In fact, as Callum and I had ridden that way so recently, we knew the ground and managed to increase our lead a little. It was becoming clear that we would need every advantage we could gain. The fast, rough riding was taking its toll on Callum. His blood soaked his trouser leg and stained the saddle fender underneath. He held on to the saddle horn as his horse made its way up the side of the valley and I could hear his laboured breathing.

We reached the top of the slope at last, but we could not afford to stop, not even to fix a bandage on Callum's leg. Below us was the sound of the four rustlers making their way up through the trees. Callum was slumped in his saddle, still clinging to the horn as we rode on. I caught a glimpse of his white face and it frightened me. We'd been riding fast for almost an hour now and Callum had been losing blood all the time. He made no sound of complaint but he was growing weaker by the minute, and he no longer had the strength to urge his tired horse on as fast as we needed to go. Then he swayed suddenly and almost fell from his saddle. His blowing horse dropped back to a walk, and I reined up beside him.

'I canna go on, laddie,' Callum said weakly. His face was damp with sweat.

'I'll tie you to your saddle,' I said, reaching for my rope.

Callum shook his head slowly. 'Ah'll keep bleedin'.' He sat a little straighter in his saddle, a look of fierce determination burning in his eyes. 'Ah'm gonna play dead. It's risky, but Ah reckon it's the best chance Ah got.'

'It's too damn risky,' I insisted.

Callum fixed me with his dark eyes. 'Ah ken a way o' putting mysel' in a trance, so it looks like Ah'm dead. Wi' any luck, they'll be happy tae see one o' us dead, an' won't bother chasin' after youse.' He pulled his gold ring off his little finger and held it out to me. 'Take care o' this, an' if ma plan dinna work, gie it tae Anne for me.'

It all seemed too risky to me, but I couldn't think of any alternative. I took the ring and slipped it into the breast pocket of my shirt. 'Good luck, Callum.' I wanted to say more, but there wasn't time.

'Doan' go too far,' Callum told me. 'Ah may be needin' youse tae help me come outta the trance.' He dismounted slowly, sliding down the side of his horse.

I thought for a moment that he was going to collapse there and then, but he kept on his feet. I took the reins of his horse, and headed across the narrow belt of open ground and into the cover of densely growing pines. I rode in sufficiently far that the horses would not be seen, and quickly tethered them where there was a small patch of grass. Moving as quiet as I could, I made my way through the trees to the point where they came closest to Callum. My caution was justified for the rustlers had turned a corner of the trail and seen Callum lying on the grass.

'That's McGeachin!' the skinny one called.

They rode up fast and dismounted, gathering around Callum like crows.

The black one looked at the blood on Callum's trousers and whistled. 'Looks like you hit him worse than you thought, Murray.' He spoke to the one who had shot Abe.

Murray crouched down, feeling Callum's throat and chest. My heart nearly stopped when the short rustler drew his pistol and aimed it point blank at Callum.

CHAPTER ELEVEN

'No need to waste your lead, Smale,' Murray told him. 'He's cashed all right.'

I swallowed hard at his words, and blinked away tears, telling myself over and over that Callum wasn't really dead.

'Are you sure?' Smale asked, giving Callum a casual kick in the ribs.

Callum lay sprawled on his back, limp and utterly unresponsive to all that was happening to him. Murray flicked open his pocket-knife and picked up Callum's hand. I winced silently as Murray pushed the tip of the knife blade under the bed of Callum's fingernail. Callum lay as still as before.

'I'm sure,' Murray answered, letting Callum's hand drop.

'What are we gonna do with him?' the black man asked. 'Mike Kershaw'll sure be glad to know

McGeachin's dead.'

Murray looked along the trail in the direction of the Diamond M. 'That 'breed that rode for the Bar S will be long gone now, especially as he took McGeachin's hoss to spell with his own. We've got no spare mount to bring this crowbait back on.'

The skinny fellow spoke up. 'Ain't this the fellow that boasted of leavin' Jake's body for the vultures to eat? I reckon we should do the same with him.'

Murray nodded. 'Seems fitting. That blood'll fetch scavengers to him in no time.' He leaned forward, knife in hand, and for a moment I thought he was about to cut open Callum's face. All he did was to saw off a lock of Callum's hair, which he put into a tobacco tin. 'You get his gunbelt, Smale. That, an' this hair should be proof enough we done caught up with him.'

Smale unfastened Callum's gunbelt, jerking it out from underneath him and rolling him over to lie face down in the grass. He pulled Callum back over again, handling him carelessly, and searched his pockets. I watched in helpless anger, and was glad that Callum had given me his ring to look after. Smale took the small amount of money he'd found and mounted up alongside his companions. They turned their horses and rode back towards the Rafter K.

I waited until they were well out of sight and earshot, then waited some more, counting slowly under my breath. Callum remained exactly as they had left him. My anxiety for him finally overcame my fear that they would return, and I left the cover of the trees to hurry to his side. I knelt down and began to examine him. His face and hands seemed cool, and when I pressed my hand to his chest, I felt no movement. My fears crowded in on me. It was possible that Callum had died from his blood loss since I'd ridden away from him. Half-panicked, I pressed my ear against his chest and listened for a heartbeat. I thought I heard one, and hope soared in me, but nothing followed. I listened longer and thought I heard another, but surely too long after the first. It could be nothing but my imagination and longing.

I raised my head and looked despairingly at his face, relaxed in death, or some strange state I didn't understand.

'Callum! Are you there, Callum?' I called. I leaned closer, trying to remember what he had said to me before we separated. 'Can you hear me?'

How was I supposed to help him to come out of his trance, if trance it was? I called his name again but he lay as still as before. I moaned in frustration, wondering what to do. Without knowing why, I touched my fingertips to his face, as he had done when healing me. Hope kindled within me for somehow I could feel that he was alive. It was faint, but there was something there that was the essence of Callum McGeachin and I had miraculously made contact with it.

'Callum, Callum.' I was breathing the words, my eyes half-closed as I tried to focus on that faint sense of his presence. 'Callum, it's Don. Come back to me. Come back to me and Anne. Callum, it's safe now. Callum, come back for me and Anne.'

I was unprepared for the sudden jolt as Callum came out of his trance. I jerked my hands away, momentarily dizzied by the force of his personality returning. Callum's chest heaved as he took a deep, gasping breath and then began to breathe more normally. His eyes opened, slowly regaining their focus as he fought his way back to full consciousness. At last, he turned his head and looked at me.

'Ah told ye it would work,' he said faintly.

Callum was still too weak to ride and in any case, the movement would have opened the wound, which had finally stopped bleeding. In spite of his protests, I picked him up and carried him into the security of the trees. There I bandaged his leg, using strips of cloth torn from an old shirt I had in my saddlebags, and left him dozing in a small patch of sunlight. I tended to the horses and foraged for wild food to add to the bread and cheese we had left. Callum woke at sunset and I was relieved to see some colour back in his face.

Moving slowly, he rested against a pine and ate, while I told him what had happened when the rustlers had found him.

'Ah wish Ah could get back tae Anne this night,' he said vehemently. 'Ah'm feart o' what can happen wi' her all alone.'

'She'll most likely be fine.' I did my best to be reassuring. 'I can't go back on my own to her. You're not fit enough to be left alone out here, and we've only the one revolver between us.'

Callum vented his frustration with a long sigh.

When it grew dark, I lit a small fire. Callum lay close to it, wrapped in the saddle blankets that were all we had in the way of bedding. He slept a little, but as night came on and the temperature dropped, I could see he was awake and shivering. There was little point in staying awake myself. I put a couple of thicker logs on the fire, to keep it burning, then settled myself on the ground beside Callum, pressed back to back. We huddled together, and as my body warmed his, he relaxed and slept.

Although he could not use his gift on himself, given rest, warmth and food, Callum had great powers of recuperation. The next morning he was weak, but able to stand and move about, and to ride. All the same, we dared not try his strength too far, and travelled no faster than a walk. It was another bright day, and Callum seemed to absorb the sunshine, drawing strength from its warmth. I rode with my hat hanging on my shoulders for a while, enjoying the liquid warmth on my straight, black hair.

It was late morning when we came in sight of the Diamond M ranch buildings. There was no sign of anybody outside, or watching for us.

'What in hell?' I was stunned to see corral posts torn down and a couple of dead hens lying not far from the kitchen door.

Callum's face went white; he kicked his horse into a gallop and raced towards the house. I followed, noticing that someone had apparently taken an axe to the water trough.

Callum hauled his horse to a halt by the kitchen door, which was hanging off its hinges, and threw himself recklessly from the saddle. He staggered on landing, and fell to his knees just outside the door. His weakness saved his life, for a rifle was fired from inside the house and the bullet passed over his head as he stumbled.

'Go away, you murderers!' Anne Molloy's voice screamed.

I did a flying dismount and raced for the open door. Callum straightened and called out.

'Anne! It's me, Callum, an' Don. Doan' shoot!'

I reached Callum and peered cautiously through the door. Anne Molloy came slowly into the kitchen from the door into the hall; she was carrying my Winchester. Her lovely face was strained and smudged with tears. I helped Callum to stand; he called Anne's name softly. She stared at him in shock as he limped towards her.

'There now, ma hen. Ah'm back for ye.' Callum spoke gently, keeping the worry from his voice. He stopped in front of Anne and caressed her cheek with his fingers. 'There's nae need tae be feart, now.'

The rifle clattered to the floor as Anne threw herself against him, almost knocking Callum off his feet. She clung to him, sobbing wildly.

'He told me you were dead! He told me you were dead!'

'Ah'm sorry, love.' Callum's words were lost into her hair.

I turned away from them, and looked about the kitchen. The makings of a pie lay abandoned on the table, the pastry dried out. I was hungry, and knew that Callum needed plenty of food to recover his strength. As I filled the kettle and put it on the stove, I began to wonder where the children were.

Anne's first hysteria had died down. She was still clinging to Callum, her arms tight around him and her cheek pressed against his as though only direct contact with his warm and living body could reassure her. I cleared my throat, and spoke quietly.

'Anne, where are the children?'

Anne moaned softly, and fear dawned on Callum's face. 'The bairns?' he asked.

'Upstairs,' Anne whispered. She released her grip on Callum and stood back to look into his face. 'Sallie's frightened, but she's not hurt.' Anne paused there, and I saw anger kindling slowly in her eyes as she told us what had happened. 'The Kershaws came here this morning, Snowy, Mike and Charlie, with some of their men. Mike showed me your gunbelt and gave me a tin with some hair in it; your hair, Callum. He told me that their men had caught you and Don stealing Rafter K cows, and you'd been shot.' She paused and swallowed. 'A man called Murray told me how he'd found you lying dead.' Anne touched his face again, reassuring herself. 'They said Don had left you to bleed to death, and run out.' She looked at me then, her clear eyes looking deep into mine. 'That was the only thing that gave me any hope. I knew that you would never abandon Callum.'

'He dinna, lassie,' Callum said, giving me a grateful look.

'Well, they wanted me to sell up to them but I wouldn't. I won't let them bully me.' Anne's voice gained strength. 'And I still had some hope you might be alive. They set their men into wrecking the place and Joey. . . .' Here she faltered. 'Joey tried to stop them, and he yelled at Mike Kershaw. He told him you were twice the man Kershaw is.

131

Then ... then Mike Kershaw lost his temper and he shot Joey.'

I could hardly believe what I heard, and felt suddenly sick.

Callum was as stunned as I was. He found his voice and asked. 'Joey? Is he dead?'

Tears spilled from Anne's eyes. 'Not yet. I couldn't leave him to find a doctor; he'd die before I got back.'

Callum straightened, his eyes shining. 'Then there's a chance.' He looked at me, inviting me to follow him as he took Anne's hand and led her up to Joey's room.

The boy had been shot in the chest, and was unconscious. Anne watched, bewildered, as Callum pulled back the sheets and examined the dying boy.

'What can you do?' she asked, hope warring with despair.

Callum covered Joey up again and turned to Anne, taking her hands in his.

'Ah've no' told ye this, ma love, because I was feart o' what ye'd think.' Slowly, Callum made his confession. 'Ah have the power tae heal in ma hands, and Ah can make Joey better. Don will tell ye Ah'm speaking the truth.'

Anne tore her gaze away from him to look at me.

I nodded. 'Callum saved my life the way he aims

to help Joey now. I don't know how he does it, but I know he has a great power within him.'

Anne looked at Callum again, then the doubt was replaced by determination. 'Do whatever you have to, to save my boy if you can.'

'I'll gie ma heart tae it,' Callum promised. He pulled Anne close for a kiss, then settled himself on a chair beside the bed.

As Callum laid his hands on Joey, Anne moved around to stand beside me and watch.

I don't know how long it took Callum to heal Joey's wounds. Almost imperceptibly, Joey's breathing grew stronger and the colour came back to his face. But as the healing went on and Joey got stronger, Callum's own strength was draining. His face was damp with sweat and his breathing became deeper and laboured. Anne was watching her son return to life, but I was getting increasingly worried for Callum. His hands started to tremble, and I moved to stand beside him. Anne's attention switched to Callum, and for the first time she noticed the bandage on his leg and the stiff coating of blood on his Levis.

At last Callum lifted his hands from Joey. He swayed as he came out of his trance and I caught him, steadying him in the chair. Callum leaned heavily against me, shaking with weakness.

'Ah've done all Ah can,' he said faintly.

Anne leaned over the bed, touching Joey on his

cheek as she spoke his name. Her son turned his head towards her and opened his eyes for a moment.

'How do you feel, Joey?' Anne asked him.

'Tired, Ma, but I don't hurt any more,' he answered drowsily.

'Rest then,' she told him, watching as he settled down.

'Callum needs rest too,' I said, and picked him up from the chair.

Callum made no protest this time as I carried him after Anne, and into her bedroom. There, I laid him on the double bed and moved aside to let Anne tend to him. I was turning to leave them when he called my name.

'Ye have something o' mine,' Callum said. He reached up for Anne's hand and pulled gently until she sat on the bed beside him. Callum was so exhausted it was an effort for him to move, but his dark eyes were bright and clear.

I knew what Callum wanted, and retrieved his gold ring from my shirt pocket. He took it and held it on the palm of his hand so Anne could see it.

'This ring was the weddin' ring o' ma great-grandmother, Lucy. She wore it from the day she were married, till the day she died. Then it was given tae her daughter, ma grandmother. The last time Ah saw her, afore I went tae take the boat tae

America, she gave it tae me an' told me tae wear it until Ah found the woman of ma heart. Anne, ye have ma heart; will ye take ma ring?'

Anne Molloy lifted her left hand and spread the fingers, looking at the two rings she already wore. Slowly, she drew off the engagement and wedding rings given to her by Tom Molloy and put them on the bedside table.

'When the children are older, I will give them these rings as keepsakes of their father. I'll wear your ring, Callum.'

Callum slipped his ring on to her finger. 'Don is witness tae our promises.'

Anne nodded, sparing me a grateful smile.

'Now bide with me a while, ma love, while I sleep,' Callum said, wrapping one arm around Anne's waist.

I knew Anne longed to stay with him, but there was doubt on her face. I guessed at the cause and spoke up.

'I'll take care of Sallie and clean up the place some. You stay with Callum.'

'Thank you, Don.' Anne allowed Callum to pull her down on to the bed beside him, and as I left the room they were wrapped in one another's arms.

CHAPTER TWELVE

'Ah reckon this spot will do,' Callum said, halting his horse.

It was the morning of the day after the Kershaws' violent visit to the Diamond M. They had told Anne they would come back the next day, so Callum and I intended to be ready for them. Callum had made plans while recovering, and now we had ridden out along the trail we expected the Kershaws to use.

Callum caught me watching him as we dismounted, and chuckled. 'Ah'm fine, Don. As Ah keep tellin' ye. Ah rested afternoon, evening and night yesterday, and ate plenty o' Anne's guid food.'

I wasn't wholly convinced, but it was true that Callum no longer limped, and was moving with much of his usual vigour.

The spot Callum had selected was a large grassy

glade between two patches of dense tree cover. Sunlight reached the middle of the open area, but under the trees, all was dim and shady. One side of the glade dipped to a hollow at the foot of a cliff. A few fallen boulders rose like islands in the grass and wild plants that covered the ground. We tethered our horses a safe distance away, made our preparations, and waited. I was lying hidden in a tangled clump of snowberry and honeysuckle, from where I could see most of the clearing. Callum was concealed among the trees where the trail left the clearing on its way to the Diamond M.

I had feared that we wouldn't be ready in time, but as we were waiting I began to worry that the Kershaws had chosen a different route to the Diamond M. Choosing this spot had been a gamble, though a carefully calculated one. Maybe an hour passed before I heard the sounds of horses approaching the far side of the clearing. I thought quickly through Callum's plan and tried to console myself with the thought that his last unlikely suggestion had worked. Then the three Kershaw brothers and four of their men rode into the clearing.

Charlie Kershaw was a little way ahead, so he was the first to see Callum. He reined his horse in sharply, staring wide-eyed into the trees ahead of him.

'What the hell?'

'McGeachin!' Mike Kershaw exclaimed.

Three of the men with them had been in the group who had pronounced Callum dead. All of them stopped their horses and stared.

Callum stood on the trail where it left the sunny clearing and entered the shadows of the trees. He wore the same clothes as the day before, including the torn Levis, caked with his own blood. His eyes glowed dark and intent from a face as pale as death. As the riders stared at him, Callum spoke in ringing tones.

'Ah ha' come fae my vengeance!'

His voice was deep and fierce, filled with power. The rustlers looked at one another uneasily. Callum thrust one hand forward, pointing at the men he faced.

'Murderrr!' He gave full vent to the rolling 'r' of his accent, flinging the word at them. 'Two souls murdered yesterday; Callum McGeachin and Joey Molloy.'

The second name caused further consternation among the Kershaws' men, and I guessed that not all of them had been told that a boy had been shot.

'Ah ha' returned frae the dead for ma vengeance!'

The horses were beginning to catch the uneasiness of their riders, tossing their heads nervously.

'It must be some kind of a trick,' Charlie blustered, staring at Callum. Mike Kershaw turned on the rustler, Murray.

'You must have been mistaken; you told me you had killed him.' He sounded uncertain in spite of his anger.

'He was dead!' Murray protested. 'I checked his body myself.'

'What if he was just unconscious?' Mike insisted, searching for a rational explanation.

'He couldn't be standing here today,' Murray said. He pointed at Callum. 'Look at all that blood. No man could bleed like that and get from Blaine Draw to here in two days, I swear it.'

'No man, but a spirit,' Callum intoned. 'A restless spirit tae strike ye down!' He flung out his arm in a dramatic gesture, and I acted on the cue.

I tugged on the end of a piece of string that ran concealed in the grass. At the other end of the string, close to the riders, a small rock fell on two detonator caps tied together. The caps exploded, scattering stones and shredded foliage. The effect on horses and riders was out of proportion to the explosion. Horses shied and barged into one another while their frightened riders cursed. Callum followed up the good work immediately.

'Ah call down a curse o' blood on youse!' he screamed, pointing directly at Murray. Callum concentrated fiercely, stretching his fingers towards the rustler, his whole body straining with effort.

Murray sat on his horse staring at Callum like a

rabbit hypnotized by a weasel. To my astonishment, I saw a thin trickle of blood start to flow from his nose. The other men noticed, and exclaimed. Murray wiped his hand across his face and stared dumbly at the blood smeared there.

'A curse o' blood,' Callum screamed again, the words tearing from his throat. 'Ah curse ye all!' He was filled with power, a white-faced, blood-drenched spirit of vengeance, capable of summoning unnatural forces.

Fear leapt like fire from one man to the next. First Smale, then two others, turned and fled. Murray might have followed them, but Snowy grabbed his horse's bridle.

'I'll show you he's no spirit!' Mike Kershaw yelled, his voice high with hysteria. He snatched his Colt from its holster, but Callum had taken advantage of the confusion to melt away into the trees bordering the trail.

I had Murray in the sights of my rifle. He had murdered my brother, and come close to killing Callum. For all that, I didn't want to pull the trigger. I didn't want to rob another human of their life. I hesitated, while Charlie swore, Mike screamed curses and the horses milled around in confusion. Watching the chaos that Callum had brought about, I realized that I would be failing him and Abe if I didn't act. I fired my rifle on the thought, and without taking proper aim.

Murray screamed, reeling in his saddle, as the bullet tore through his shoulder. Mike Kershaw fired his revolver into the woods, though nowhere near either me or Callum. Charlie had drawn his gun too, and was searching for someone to shoot. I'd given Callum my Army Peacemaker, and I heard it firing a little way around the edge of the clearing from where I was. Mike Kershaw's horse squealed and half-reared, hit in the chest.

Charlie and Snowy were both firing into the trees. Murray turned his mount and tried to escape, clutching his bleeding shoulder with one hand. Charlie turned on him, yelling curses.

'Stand and fight, you yellow-bellied cur!' He fired a shot past Murray's head. 'I'll shoot you myself if you run.'

Mike's horse was beginning to collapse beneath him. Its eyes rolled in pain and fear as he hauled on the reins to try and keep it up. I didn't know whether Callum had intended to shoot the horse or the man, but I shot to finish the horse off. Its legs buckled and Mike kicked himself clear of the stirrups to slide clear as the dying horse hit the ground.

'Take cover,' grunted Snowy, bending in his saddle to reach for Mike.

A shot from Callum tore Snowy's grey hat off as Snowy leaned over.

Murray saw the hollow at the foot of the cliff,

and made for that. Snowy swung Mike up behind him and followed. Charlie threw another shot into the trees, then found his revolver empty. He turned his horse on its hocks, thrusting the gun back into its holster, and raced after the others. I heard Callum fire again, and took another shot myself. My blood was up now, and I fired twice more as the Kershaws raced for the cover of the hollow. I saw Mike flinch as a bullet grazed his ribs, and wanted to whoop with pride and excitement.

They abandoned their horses at the edge of the hollow, taking rifles and scrambling down on foot to vanish from my line of sight. I glanced away and saw Callum running from the cover of the trees into the clearing. I got up too, dashing out through the grass while the Kershaws and Murray were settling themselves into the hollow. Their frightened horses had kept on galloping, disappearing among the trees. Callum was aiming for a pair of rocks standing together some twenty feet from the edge of the hollow, and I swerved that way to join him. Already, a rifle barrel was showing over the rim of the hollow, as the Kershaws prepared to defend themselves. I dived the last few feet into the cover of the rocks, landing alongside Callum. A rifle bullet cracked just behind me as I hit the dirt.

Callum grinned at me as he recovered his breath after the run. He looked odd close to, for I had dusted his face with flour earlier to achieve the ghostly skin colour of an undead spirit.

'Ma ruse worked,' he said with a touch of pride. 'Ah wanted tae cut the odds against us, an' those three were so feart, they never fired a shot.'

'I'm sure glad you're on my side,' I answered wholeheartedly.

I peered around the side of my rock, and withdrew hurriedly. A shot from the hollow missed my head by inches and flattened itself on the reddish stone. Callum looked thoughtful.

'Stalemate,' he muttered, checking the loads in his revolver.

'We'll be up the creek without a paddle iffen those three do come back, with or without their friends,' I warned.

The Kershaws may have been thinking along the same lines, but they had the disadvantage of having two injured men with them.

'McGeachin!' It was Mike Kershaw yelling. 'I'm gonna shoot you myself, and I'll make sure you damn well stay dead.'

'An' you're the man so brave ye shot a nine-year old child,' Callum responded, loathing clear in his voice.

'I should have shot both the damn kids,' Mike called. 'I should have had their mother too. I always wanted to know what it would be like to have Anne Molloy underneath me. I bet she's a whore in her bedroom.'

'Doan' youse talk about her that way!' Callum roared, brittle with fury.

Mike Kershaw laughed mockingly. 'I'll go an' take her when I've killed you, McGeachin. I'll throw your body in front of her, then I'll tear her clothes off and show her what it's like to have a real man in her bed.'

Callum shuddered and I thought he was about to rise and charge recklessly into the fire of the rifles that would be waiting. I grabbed his shoulder, feeling how tight his muscles were as he fought to contain his anger.

'Don't fall for it,' I hissed.

Charlie's voice joined in now.

'We'll take turns with her. She'll be too exhausted to weep for you, McGeachin.'

Callum gave a low moan, something between disgust and fury. His eyes burned with the fierce power that welled up within him, so strong and dangerous I began to feel afraid. He looked up at the cliff above the hollow where the Kershaws were hiding.

'Don, do ye see that overhang in the rock there, about thirty feet up?'

I followed his gaze. 'There's a bent pine growing from the top of it?'

'Aye, an' aneath the overhang there's a crack runnin' tae the right.'

144

'I see it.' I was puzzled, but willing to find out what Callum planned.

'Take a guid aim at that crack wi' yer rifle, an' be ready tae shoot when Ah tells ye,' he ordered.

I took aim as I was told, concentrating hard to block out my thoughts and Callum's powerful presence beside me. From the corner of my vision, I saw him placing his hands flat against the rock he was sheltering behind. Mike Kershaw was shouting something again, but now Callum was oblivious. It felt as though an electric storm was brewing very close. My skin tingled and my heart was pounding. I squinted along the barrel of my Winchester, waiting for the moment, waiting for the storm to break.

'Shoot!' The single word burst from Callum.

I snatched the trigger, but my aim was true. The bullet hit the cliff face in the crack just beneath the overhang. Callum gave a wordless cry as he pushed against the rock in front of him. The overhang began to split away from the cliff, then suddenly the cliff face seemed to be moving, breaking and falling. More pieces shattered away, crashing down into the hollow. I heard screams from the men in there, cries of terror as rocks and trees plummeted towards them. Those screams froze me as lighter stones and dust billowed out from the pile of debris.

A moan from Callum broke through my shock.

I turned to see him leaning against the rock, white-faced and breathing heavily. The tips of his fingers were bleeding from being pressed so hard against the rock as he unleashed his power. I was about to speak his name, when I heard stones rattling against one another, and knew that someone had survived. I hurriedly worked the lever action of my rifle and popped up from cover. There was still so much dust in the air I couldn't see anything at first. Then I glimpsed someone running away, heading for the trees. I got off a couple of shots but neither hit. He got among the trees and vanished in the direction of the Rafter K. I looked back at the mass of rock and debris filling the hollow, and saw no other signs of life.

I crouched beside Callum, who was recovering from his incredible efforts.

'Did ye see who it was?' he asked.

I shook my head. 'That fall brought down a lot of dust. How much of that did you cause, Callum? How in hell did you start a rock fall?'

'Youse started it,' Callum said. 'Ah helped it; an' it wasna' easy,' he added, rubbing his forehead and leaving smudges of blood. He studied his raw fingertips for a moment, then gave a long sigh. 'Ah reckon we'd best gang an' see what we've done.'

We found Murray and Snowy Kershaw, both crushed to death by the rock fall. I stared at Murray's body and remembered Abe, my brother.

'You won't kill anyone else now,' I said to Murray's body. A weight seemed to lift from me, and I knew that what we had done was justified.

We also found Charlie Kershaw, pinned by a slab of rock that had crushed him from the waist to the knees. He was still conscious, though barely, exchanging his moans for curses as we knelt either side of him. Callum examined him, ignoring Charlie's feeble attempts to brush him away, then shook his head.

'Ah canna help,' he said, more to me than to Charlie.

'Damn you,' Charlie hissed, his face screwed up in agony.

Callum had his left hand on Charlie's forehead. He concentrated briefly, and Charlie slipped into unconsciousness. Callum looked across his body at me.

'Even if we could get this rock off of him, Ah doan' reckon Ah could save him. The only thing Ah can do for him is tae help him go quickly; tae release him frae his body.'

'You mean shoot him?' I asked.

Callum shook his head. 'No, laddie. His kin will be comin' tae find him, an' while they'll no' want him tae suffer, they won't forgive us for shooting him like a horse wi' a broken leg neether. If Ah release his spirit, they'll never ken he died o' anythin' besides his injuries.' Callum spoke with

147

determination, but I felt that he was uneasy about what he intended to do.

'Go ahead, if you think it's right,' I told him.

Callum shifted his position so he could cradle Charlie's face in both hands. He took in a slow, deep breath, and went into a trance.

As I watched, Charlie's breathing became shallower. I thought it would be over quickly, but Callum's body was tense with effort and he started to moan. Fear crept into my heart as I watched him struggle. He shook, his breath coming in ragged gasps, and sweat plastered strands of hair to his face. As I watched, I suddenly understood: in spite of his injury, Charlie was stubbornly clinging to life. Callum's instinct was to heal, not end life, and his own conflict weakened him.

Fury at Charlie filled me: fury at all the wrongs done to Callum and the Molloys, fury at Charlie's spitefulness. I impulsively placed my hands over Callum's, feeling a jolt as he somehow made contact with me. Seizing my anger, he exerted his will and overcame Charlie's resistance. The fierce tension suddenly vanished.

Callum slumped against me, shaking. 'Thank ye,' he whispered.

'Come and rest over here,' I said, helping him move into the sunshine. His face was pale, even where the flour had rubbed off, but I was relieved to see a quick flash of his impish grin.

'Did ye bring the whiskey, lad? As sure could use a wee drop now.'

I fetched the hipflask and we both drank, as once again, birds began to chatter and sing in the trees. I held my hand out in front of me.

'Am I a healer too?'

Callum frowned as he thought. 'Ah doan' know. Ye ha' a power, that's for sure, but maybe not for healin'. Some folk ha' power in their voices, or their eyes. They can see what others canna see.'

'I'm certain sure I can't see the future,' I replied. 'But . . . sometimes . . . more often now . . . I can feel what a person really thinks. But I don't always know what I think myself.'

Callum chuckled. 'Aye, it's a wise man that knows himself.'

And Callum was never less than true to himself.

CHAPTER THIRTEEN

We returned to the Diamond M as soon as Callum had recovered enough to sit on his horse. Anne and Sallie were waiting for us, their faces bright with worry and hope. Callum slid down from his saddle and took Anne into his arms.

'All's well, ma love, all's well,' he reassured her. 'Now Ah maun rest.' Anne put her arm around his shoulders and helped him inside.

There was no opportunity to talk more to Callum about the power I had found in myself. He had little energy to spare for anything beside sleeping and eating, and I was busy repairing the damage done by the Kershaws. The day after our confrontation, I rode into Ridgeway to find out what news there was from the Rafter K, and to make the arrangements for Callum and Anne to marry. My arrival in town caused something of a sensation, as I told them when I returned to the

150

ranch in the late evening.

'Some hands from the Rafter K had stopped in town on their way to pastures new,' I reported, sitting comfortably in the parlour. 'They told wild stories about Callum's ghost returning to wreak vengeance on the Rafter K.'

Callum, curled lazily on the sofa against Anne, grinned impishly.

I continued. 'No one in Ridgeway could tell anything about who had murdered Callum, or why he'd cursed the Rafter K, but I swear some of them were plumb disappointed when I told them you were still alive. I reckon they took to the idea of murder and blood, and wanted to tell their grandchildren the story.'

Callum looked up into Anne's face. 'We'll ha' a guid enough story tae tell our grandchildren, hen. An' the folk will see Ah'm alive well enough in three days, when we gang tae town for tae get married.'

Anne smiled and brushed his hair with her lips. Sometimes I remember that moment, and I ache a little inside.

Callum McGeachin and Anne Molloy were married by a Justice of the Peace in Ridgeway. I was there as witness, along with Joey and Sallie, and the Hitchin family from the DH Connected. Callum was dressed up in black town trousers, a white shirt and his black frockcoat with a fancy double-breasted waistcoat underneath. I'd noticed him limping the night before, when tired, but now he was all pepped up with happiness. Anne wore a fine cream dress, trimmed with blue ribbon that matched her eyes. She wore her long dark hair braided and coiled into a mat on the back of her head, with tiny blue flax flowers tucked among the glossy coils. As fine as she looked, the most beautiful thing about her was the glow in her eyes as she looked at Callum.

When the short ceremony was over, I revealed the surprise I had organized for them. I'd sent for a photographer to come from Ouray and he took half a dozen plates outside on the grass out front of the stores. Beautiful pictures they turned out to be: Callum with his unruly hair ruffled by the breeze, standing beside his elegant lady. They are pictures full of love and hope. Afterwards there was a wedding breakfast at the restaurant where they had first met. Folk from the town dropped in to wish them well, and I suspect to see the man who was the subject of so much wild rumour. Callum laughed, joked and even sang for us as we celebrated.

The meal was about finished when a boy came scurrying in and sidled up to Callum.

'There's a message for you from the livery,' the boy said, his eyes on the remains of the food spread on the tables. 'Mr Browne says as one of your team horses has got the colic something bad.'

Callum thanked the freckle-faced boy and gave him a piece of white-frosted wedding cake. He still smiled but it was plain to see the news had made him uneasy. Callum turned to Anne and said quietly.

'Ah'm just goin' tae see about the horse. It shouldna' take long afore Ah'm back.'

He gave her a swift kiss on the cheek and rose, inviting me to accompany him.

We turned the corner at the end of the block and walked past the bank.

Ridgeway was quiet, with hardly another person to be seen on the wide street. Two burros waited patiently outside the saloon, dozing beneath their heavy packs.

'Ah doan know how the horse can get colic,' Callum remarked, walking briskly. 'Unless Browne gie it a feed afore watering. Anyhow, Ah want tae see the beastie's all right.'

My attention was caught by a display of guns in the window of the store we were passing, and I stopped to look. Callum's gun and belt were still at the Rafter K, so far as we knew, but there was a new Colt Thunderer in the window.

'I'll catch up in a minute,' I promised, trying to see the price of the gun.

'A' right.' Callum kept on walking, his thoughts

no doubt more on the sick horse we were going to see.

I found the price of the revolver and made a mental note to tell Callum about it later.

He had drawn a few yards ahead of me, and jumped down off the sidewalk to cross the street. I followed, and as I reached the edge of the sidewalk, a sudden movement on the far side of the street caught my eye. A man burst from the alleyway between two buildings, raising a pistol towards Callum as he crossed the street. I grabbed for my own revolver and screamed a warning.

'Callum!'

'McGeachin!' It was Mike Kershaw, out for revenge.

Callum hesitated, momentarily confused by the two shouts. He started to turn towards Kershaw, his hand automatically dropping to where his gun should have been. Kershaw fired once, and Callum stumbled backwards, crumpling on to the dirt surface of the street.

I was much further from Mike Kershaw than he was from Callum. He was at long range for my Colt, but I raised the gun to shoulder level and aimed before firing. There was no hesitation in anything I did. I fired, and Mike Kershaw in turn was thrown back against the wall behind him. As he slid to the ground, I leapt on to the street and raced across to him, my gun held ready in my hand. I only needed to get within a few feet of him to see that he was dead, head-shot. His eyes were open and blank, life snatched abruptly away. I felt no emotion over killing him.

Whirling around, I thrust my gun back into its holster and ran to where Callum lay. He was on his back, his right hand pressed against his chest. Blood seeped between his fingers and spread in a bright stain across his white shirt. Callum was coughing, choking on the blood that bubbled from his mouth and nose. I pulled off my black hat and slipped it gently under his head. Callum coughed again and spat blood but with his head raised, he could breathe more freely. I pressed my hand over his, knowing it would do nothing to stop the fatal bleeding.

'I'm sorry, Callum,' I said futilely. 'I didn't see him in time.'

Callum's eyes were hazed with pain as he struggled to breathe. 'Ah didna' see him neither.' His eyes cleared then, looking intently into mine. Once again we connected and I felt everything in him: the regret at having to leave before he was ready, the disappointment, the anger at Mike Kershaw and the pleasure at his death, his gratitude to me. Above all, bright and warm, was his love for Anne, wrapped in all the things he'd want to tell her, to share with her. I sensed memories – people and places from his past that I didn't know, but Anne was in the forefront of his mind, and I knew what he wanted from me, and how I could use my power to help.

'I'll tell her everything,' I promised.

Callum let his eyes close, and his body relaxed as his life ebbed away. He breathed a few times more, then his chest sank under my hands and didn't rise again.

I watched numbly as things happened around me after that. Someone must have told Anne what had happened, for she came running down the street, the skirt of her wedding dress hitched up to run faster. I watched as she cradled Callum's head in her lap, silent tears of shock dropping on to his hair. Anne wiped the blood from his face with the sleeve of her dress, uncaring of the red stain on the cream fabric. Someone told me that the Hitchins were taking care of Joey and Sallie. Other voices spoke of Mike Kershaw, and of Callum. Mike Kershaw had paid the boy to take the message to Callum. It had been a trap, born of jealousy and hate. The voices discussed what should be done now, sending for the sheriff and the preacher.

At last, Anne McGeachin bent her head and kissed her husband on the lips in farewell. I picked Callum up for the last time, cradling him in my arms like a sleeping child. With Anne walking beside me, I carried Callum's body to his coffin.

EPILOGUE

I kept my promise to Callum and stayed with Anne at the Diamond M for nearly three years. We grieved together, and built up the ranch that Callum had fought for. Eventually, when the ranch business was stable and Anne had good men to work for her, I left to roam and seek my own destiny. I returned occasionally to the Diamond M, for the people there were the closest to a family I had. Not so long ago, I went back to fulfil my role in that family.

I rode in from the south on a bright spring day, much like when I had first seen this valley. I did not go directly to the sprawling ranch, but rode higher along the side of the valley, just below the tree line. The place I was looking for was as I remembered it, a small, gently sloping meadow cut into the valley side above the ranch. Pine and aspen sheltered the alpine meadow from the east, and to the west was a glorious view across the valley. This was where we had laid Callum to rest, his body watched over by the mountains he had loved. The simple wooden grave marker I had made still stood in spite of the winter snows.

As I approached, I saw someone standing by the grave marker, tracing his finger around the worn letters carved there:

CALLUM MCGEACHIN
HEALER

It was a black-haired boy, sturdy though small for his thirteen years. He looked around as he heard my horse's hooves, and his face broke into an impish grin, revealing the gap between his front teeth.

'Uncle Don!' he exclaimed happily.

I dismounted and greeted Scott McGeachin. It was four years since I had last seen him and my heart ached to see how much he was growing to resemble Callum, the father he'd never known. Scott had been born almost nine months after his father's death, a gift to console those Callum had had to leave behind.

'How are your family, Scott?' I asked.

'They're swell,' Scott replied. 'Sallie's getting wedded to Rob Hitchin sometime around the fourth of July.'

'That's good news,' I said. I looked at the grave marker Scott had been studying.

'Why are you up here?' I asked gently.

Scott turned to look at his father's grave marker. 'I . . . I wanted to talk to him. I've been dreaming about him at nights. I only know my father from those wedding pictures but I see him so clearly in my dreams. I hear him, too. '*Dinna be feart, Scott, Ah'll be wi' ye when ye come tae yer power.*'

I shivered at the uncanny way Scott had reproduced his father's speech. The boy had never heard Callum's Scots tongue. Scott was staring at me curiously.

'Is that the way he spoke?' he asked.

I nodded. 'Callum was speaking to you.'

Scott's dark eyes widened as he considered this. 'Don, do you know what he meant by my "power"?' He paused and continued. 'I feel sometimes . . . as if I. . . .'

This was why I had returned now. Scott was on the verge of manhood, and the power that ran in the McGeachins was growing strong in him now as his body changed. Standing close to him, I could feel it close within his conscious reach.

'I know what you mean,' I reassured the youngster. 'I was like you when Callum found me, and he woke me to my potential. Yours will come naturally and I will teach you what I can.'

Scott stared at me, half-believing but unsure. I

held out my hands towards him, and after a brief hesitation, he took them. He gasped slightly as he felt my power, and started to gain some idea of his own potential. After a few moments, I released him. Scott stood lost in wonder for a minute before speaking.

'Does Ma know about this power? My father had it, didn't he?'

'Yes. Callum used his gift to save Joey's life, and mine before that.'

A look of astonishment dawned on Scott's face. He spun around to stare at the grave marker. 'Healer! Now I understand why you put "healer" on his grave. And I will be a healer man too.' He stood there, the sunlight bright on his black hair as he made his vow.

To help him keep that vow will be my last duty to Callum. Now I watch over his boy, loving Scott McGeachin as I had loved his gallant father, and I am content.